HAVE I BEEN OVER-WED?

HAVE I BEEN OVER-WED?

A Boulevard of Broken Dreams

Renooka Gopaul

authorHOUSE®

AuthorHouse™
1663 Liberty Drive
Bloomington, IN 47403
www.authorhouse.com
Phone: 1-800-839-8640

First published by AuthorHouse   08/25/2011

ISBN: 978-1-4567-8847-6 (sc)
ISBN: 978-1-4567-8846-9 (ebk)

Printed in the United States of America

Any people depicted in stock imagery provided by Thinkstock are models, and such images are being used for illustrative purposes only.
Certain stock imagery © Thinkstock.

This book is printed on acid-free paper.

CONTENTS

Chapter

PROLOGUE:
The Sea Of Memories

The sun was shining brightly on the little pool of water near my veranda, the result of heavy rain in the last few days. I could see small bits of stones glisten in the muddy water like pearls. Looking at them stirred something deep inside my heart, something that has pained me for years, and has left me fatigued and tired. I started to feel lonely. I had no work to keep myself busy since it was a Sunday. "God", I said to myself, "A little longer in this little flat without any work is going to choke me till death." I decided I couldn't just sit there and let myself drown in a sea of memories—memories which have terrorized me and tortured me so often. I rose, dressed myself in the clothes lying on my bedside, and headed to the bus-stop. I boarded a bus to Alexandra Palace, a fairly short ride from my home.

I got down from the bus, walked purposelessly down the narrow road till I found a bench to sit. Sitting there idly, I could see four little boys playing in the small stretch of grassy land not too far away from me. It was as if we were from different worlds. For me, time had stopped moving and seconds seemed hard to pass by; the kids were engrossed in childish playfulness and vibrant laughter, as time seemed to run with them, spreading lots of youthful energy around them.

It must have been a few minutes that I had been watching them play, enjoying their every move and trying to get a feel of their joy, silently smiling to myself. The boys seemed to be aware of my presence, and the keen yet quiet interest I had taken in their games. They were looking towards me every now and then, saying something to each other. Suddenly, the youngest one of them, who must have been about 4 years old, ran towards me, and said "Ma'am, would you please play with us?" pointing to his little football. "Our parents are lying there and listening to music, and are not willing to play with us. But we are a player short." I was delighted to receive the offer—something hidden inside me lit up—something that was childish and was long buried—something that inspired me to jump around, play, and laugh like a little girl. I said "Yes darling", and saw his lips bend into a wide smile. Children are like angels who can make you forget all your sorrow for a moment with just a cute smile.

As I approached the little boy I saw his parents looking at me suspiciously from the distance. I gave them an assuring look as if to say that I was harmless. They watched me laughing and playing with their kids for a few minutes, and then they decided likewise. After a while, when it was time for them to go back home, the small boy came up to me and said "Thank you ma'am for playing with us. Wish I could have stayed longer. Please play with us the next day too." I smiled and said "Sure!" His parents were close behind. They came up to me and thanked me for the time I had spent with their kids. "You are a wonderful lady", said the lady, "You were so happy playing with our children, and you don't even know them." I smiled and said "Oh I love playing with children. They remind me of my childhood." The lady smiled. "You must be having a lot of fun at home with your children" said the gentleman.

The seemingly harmless question seemed to have pierced my ears and my heart broke into pieces. I was lost for a moment, but I pulled myself together and answered with a wry smile "I don't have any children". They spotted the pain in my eyes. "Sorry", said the gentleman, "It must be difficult to live on your own, especially when you are such a caring woman." I nodded. "May God bless you", he continued, "and gives you all the happiness you wish for."

The little boy was too tired from playing to stay there anymore. He started to tug at his father's pants saying "I want to go home, Papa. Please." They agreed. All the children and their parents waved me good bye and left. As the happy family vanished from my sight, a familiar feeling grabbed me. I started feeling lonely again, as if something precious was being taken away from me and I could do nothing. I could hear my inner voice cry out loud "How can I be happy when my past haunts me all the time? How can I hide my miserable life and forget about it? How can I be a happy woman, when my heart bleeds from past wounds and I can't do anything about it? How can I run away from the fact that behind that smile of mine I have hid years of sorrow and suffering? How can I?"

These questions were not new to me; they had now become a part of my existence—if I could even call this life of mine 'existence' anymore. I started to feel weak in the knees. The cloud of memories from a sorry past started surrounding me and blurred my vision. I could not even say for sure if I was awake or dreaming. Either way, this was a nightmare, one I have learnt to fear for a few years now. Yes, the sea of memories had finally drowned me in its deepest waters!

CHAPTER-1:
My Tryst With Poverty

I was born on the 3rd of December 1953, a Thursday, at 11am in Mauritius. My parents named me Pearl and welcomed me into a poor family of five children. All five were girls, and my father was the only earning member of the family. A lorry driver by profession, it was very difficult for him to provide us with the basic amenities even. My mother used to stay back home and take care of a few cows, arrange for the grass, feed them, clean the stable and look after the kids. In those times, women were not supposed to work or bring money home.

As days, months and years passed by, I was growing up amidst a world of poverty. Wherever I went, I used to hear people talking about how unlucky it was to give birth to a girl. The parents have to feed her till she was grown up, and then find a husband for her, which cost a lot at that time. I used to get very sad, and told my parents about what I overheard. They consoled me, but I could tell from their eyes that whatever people said was true. I used to be shocked at the way people thought of boys as profit and girls as loss. Gradually I was becoming accustomed to the notion that being born as a girl was a curse.

Meanwhile, when I was a couple of years old, another child was welcomed into the family. This time the baby was a boy. It was a moment of relief for my parents, especially after having given birth to five girls before. My dad was delighted. He knew that when the boy would grow up, he would look after his parents, earn for them, and take over the family's responsibility when the time would be ripe.

When I was four years old, I started going to nursery school. All my sisters were in the primary school then and I could hardly wait to get promoted to primary school as well. I was very fond of school, of making friends with a lot of class-mates, and of learning about life that was beyond the unforgiving walls of poverty. Soon I was fed up of how long it was taking me to go to primary school.

I had this funny feeling that a year was an awfully long time to wait. I could hardly wait for the New Year and other festivals to come around over again. As was the custom, we had to celebrate every festival with utmost religious sincerity; otherwise people would laugh at us and call us outcasts. Being part of a pious society, especially a poor one, we could hardly afford that. Hence my parents used to save fifty cents out of dad's weekly wages, so that they could buy new clothes for the kids and other religious necessities at the time of festivals.

As I was growing up, I could see my life changing. Being the youngest child of all, I used to be the centre of attraction for the family; now that my brother was here, the love of my family was being shared. I felt sad and was jealous of my brother; but I was mature enough to keep it to myself. I realized that if I expressed my feelings, difficulties would mount on my family, leaving all of us shattered. I told myself that I should try to be a good girl, and have a clear mind and a soft heart, and always be loved. So I was, by my parents, siblings, relatives, neighbours, teachers and everyone else. I thoroughly enjoyed the love I received from all of them.

At a modest age of five years, I started attending primary school. I was delighted to be honest; the long wait was finally over. However, there were complications that would soon crush my delight. Two of my sisters were already 12 and 13 years old, and my parents decided that it was time for them to stop attending school. In those days, secondary school used to be for boys only. Unless you were rich enough to afford private tuition for the girls, there was no way that they would be able to continue their studies.

Poverty had always been the driving factor in our family; it was the same this time around too. My sisters' education had come to a dead end. I was extremely sad at their plight, and promised to myself that someday I would break free of the shackles that held girls at home and stopped them from going out to work and earn. I could not tolerate the mindless laws which presumed that girls are weak, and therefore they should never go out alone on the streets. A silent fire of rebellion had started burning inside me, ever since I joined primary school.

My results spoke against my resolve. At the end of the first year in school, I came fifth in the class. I was extremely disappointed, and decided that I had to study harder and better my results. Life at school and beyond was beginning to open up to me. I loved to play with my friends and siblings after school every day, and the cherished the fun we had together. The second year brought better news—I had come first in my class. I was delighted! I promised myself that that I would work harder and harder every year to keep up with the good results. Gradually I could notice that I was evolving into a mature, ambitious woman. Unlike my sisters, I wanted to go out for higher education, and maybe one day, get myself a job to help my father.

Bit by bit, our family was growing into a large one. Now we were ten siblings, eight sisters and two brothers. Those were days when "population explosion" was unheard of, and big families like ours were perfectly normal. I loved having so many siblings; but I was equally worried about how tough it was becoming for my parents to cope up with the pressure. It was never easy to feed ten kids and then pay for the education of half of them. Nevertheless, I enjoyed a very close relationship with my mum and believed that I had a special place in her heart.

I was doing pretty well at school. I was now in my sixth year at primary school. Soon I classified for the seventh year because of my consistently good performance. This was a special class called "labourse" and my final hurdle before getting into secondary school. The first five students with the best results would qualify for free secondary school. The rat race was difficult, since all other parents arranged for private tuitions for their kids, which my parents could not afford. I tried my best with whatever I had in me. Every morning before the exams, I would pray to the Almighty saying "Please help me get really good results. I want to carry on with my studies so that I can reward my parents for everything they have done for me."

But it was not to be. When the results came out, I found that I was not among the top five students. I was heartbroken, and lost my self-belief completely. I went back home, drenched in a pool of tears, and announced my failure to my parents. They tried to console me and explained that it was not possible to get everything one wants in her life. As the year ended, they stated the obvious to me—it wasn't possible for me to continue with my studies since they could not afford it anymore. I would get up and cry every morning, pleading to them like a little girl to send me to secondary school. I would promise them that I would give it everything I had, that I would not disappoint them, that I would help them with the expenses once I got a job. But they refused.

Years rolled by and soon it was 1966. Nothing had changed in my life. I would cry myself to sleep every life hoping against hope that something would make my life change. Finally, the One above all listened to my prayers. A few days later, my mum was employed as a labourer. Now the family earnings had increased, and I could afford to go to secondary school. I was delighted like I had never been before! Frantic in my gaiety, I promised myself that I would leave no stone unturned, and would push myself to the limits to finally get a good job and reduce the burden of my parents.

During the first three months at secondary school, I had no problem in paying my fees of Rs.12. But after that, I used to be late every month. Family pressure had started to tell on my parents. I would be sent to the principal's office every month to explain the situation. Before long, it became a habit for me to go up to him and tell him that we are poor. My classmates would laugh at my humiliation, but I never bothered. I knew better than to be ashamed of my poverty. I was proud of my parents since I knew how hard they worked every day to look after our family.

The year ended soon enough, and I stood ninth in my class, not a bad performance considering that all other classmates took private tuition. At January, my parents sat down with me and explained that they could no longer afford my school. My brother had reached the age for secondary school, and it was impossible to bear the education expenses of two children simultaneously. I was disheartened.

So my brother started school, but in just two weeks, he backed out. He was not interested in further studies. I saw my opportunity. I begged my parents to let me resume school, to which they finally agreed. The very next morning, I prepared myself with renewed vigour and accompanied my mum to a school, only to find that there were no vacancies. My flying hopes were shattered once again. I told my mum that I had come to terms with the fact that God didn't want to help me. Mum understood my pain, and said that I shouldn't lose hope just yet. God will be there for me at the right time.

The next morning, we received a guest at our house. He was a certain Christian priest. It was perfectly normal for priests to pay us house visits; however, none of us had seen this particular priest ever before. He was rather inquisitive, and seeing me at home asked my mum straightaway why I wasn't at school. Mum told him we were poor and that there were no vacancies even if they could afford school. He made a sorry face but soon came up with an idea. He told me to come for admission to a school which was run by the Church. My hopes were rising once again, as I was back to school. But that wouldn't be the end of my miseries. Soon enough, my parents were finding it difficult to pay the Rs.14 monthly fees. I was late as usual, and the humiliation continued. Only half of the year had been over when my parents told me that my second brother would be eligible for secondary school the following year. I knew there was room for only one of us, and as a girl, I was supposed to make the sacrifice.

For me, the last few days at school were like gold-dust. I was determined to make the most of whatever time was remaining. Time flew real fast, and soon it was the end of the year. Tears had replaced the glow of happiness in my eyes once again. In November 1967, one of my sisters got married. The pressure of household work mounted on the younger sisters now that the eldest was gone. Being at home, I had to help my mum and other sisters with the chores, and also look after the youngest sister who was just one year old. I loved kids and happily took the responsibility, since I knew that the other sisters were not as patient with kids as I was.

I was aware that my dad liked to play the lottery a lot, with the hope of winning something someday. I used to hope so too and always dreamt of a day when my dad would win some money and I would be able to resume studies. Days, months, and years rolled. Nothing happened. I was of eighteen now, and was maturing into this lady who had come to terms with whatever she could never have in her life.

CHAPTER-2:
Becoming A Lady

The day, 12th March, 1968 on which Mauritius achieved its much sought independence was a red letter day in my life of fifteen years. The then Prime Minister, Sir Seewoosagur Ramgoolam gave the Chinese authority to make investments in our country. As a result, they established various types of industries in Mauritius amongst which the number of textile industries is mentionable. I have already become much matured to realise that things won't change in our poverty stricken family and I have to draw the finish line to my studies.

So, with the help of helping my family a bit and also to stand on my own legs, I sought permission from my dad so that he let me work in one of the textile factories. As expected, he was reluctant at first as people in those days were not so westernized to let their daughters work in factories. But finally he had to give up before my pleadings and wish and he let me join the factory on one condition that my two elder sisters will also accompany me to work. I started a new chapter of my life by taking up a job of production clerk at the "Floreal Knitwear" on 15th June in the year of 1972.

As I had no other work to do, I went on working in the factory 5-6 days per week and tried to support my parents financially as much as I could. Due to my hard work, dedication and perseverance, my boss was quite pleased and I was promoted to the post of production clerk in the pressing section.

A year later, a young man joined the same factory as a timekeeper. He appeared to be quite interested in me and always used to give a smile whenever we came across. Due to the necessity of his job, he had to come to the section opposite to the one in which I was posted. For this reason, I got so much used in seeing him that if he didn't turn up for a single day, I would wonder where he had been. After a couple of weeks, it came to my notice that the name written on my Identity Card was wrong. So, I went to that timekeeper guy and he I could feel that he tried to flirt with me while rectifying the mistake by saying that he is extremely sorry to make a mistake on the card of the most beautiful girl in the factory! I kept on pondering whether the mistake was intentionally done but kept my thoughts to myself only.

My elder sister was going to England in July of 1973 and my sister went to the British embassy at Port Louis for completing the formalities regarding paperwork. There my family met a gentleman named Rob, who had expressed his desire to marry me when I was only 13 in the year1967. Actually he came to see my sister as a formality of arranged marriage and had his eyes on me. But my parents didn't accept the proposal as both he and I were too young. He agreed to wait and that he went to the same place as ours to collect his visa. And when he met my parents, he brought back the proposal again. The very next day, he came right to our house to ask for my hand. My parents agreed easily as they took it to be granted that this was what destiny held for us. He said that he would be leaving for Germany in two days so it will be better if my parents gave us the permission to get engaged before he left. He came to me next day and said lovingly that he will be very sincere and loyal and will take good care of me after marriage. He would come back as early as possible as he would miss me.

In the following day, I along with my mom and sister went to see him off at the airport. Before leaving, he handed me 10

Rupees with which I decided to buy an idol of the Hindu God, Rama and Sita and pray before it every day for his well-being. One night, I realised my folly that though I had made a big commitment of lifetime, I don't have any feelings for him. But I kept mum because everybody in my family was happy.

After three days had passed, I received a letter and card from him informing that he had reached Luxembourg safely and he had been missing me all the way along and also there. It bore no address so I could not reply back. A few days later, I again received a letter from him which said that he had met a girl from my nation there and he is going on a date with her as a friend. I didn't feel jealous at that but I don't know why my mind started getting filled with bad thoughts. Panic started gripping me but still I had no way to lighten my burden as I still didn't have any address to reply back to him.

I continued to do my job as if nothing unusual had happened. The timekeeper whose name turned out to be Goldie was still interested in me. One day, I was handed over a letter by a friend, Jocelyne. It was from Goldie who had written that he was madly in love with me and wanted to have a talk with me. I kept silent and smiled to myself. On the same day, after I returned home my mom handed over me a letter which came in my name. I went to a quiet place and opened that only to be shocked at its content. It went on like this:

Hi how are you? I am fine; I just wanted to let you know that I have changed my mind. I am not coming back and I would like to tell you that my love was "une riviere sans retour".

I didn't know how to face my parents and make them confront the truth so I kept on crying to myself and fell asleep. I woke up fresh next morning and thanked God for saving me from the jaws of marriage with a person whom I didn't love. I gave the letter to my mom and after going through it, she said that she happy too as she had been feeling that I was going well off with this marriage.

All day I kept pondering over Goldie's letter and my heart said that I was falling in love for the first time in my life at just 19 years of age. Later on, that day, I told my friends that I would be replying Goldie back. I wrote him a letter saying that I too feel the same for him and agreed to go on a date after work time was over to the town of Curepipe. It was a Saturday and the first date of my life on 25th August, 1973. I was above the ninth cloud!

As my elder sisters used to work in the same factory as mine, I had to hide the entire matter from them because I knew that if they told my father about all these, he would surely stop me from going to work anymore. So, I sought the help of one of my friend, Bibi by asking her to convince my parents by saying that we should be going for shopping in the town coming Saturday. Thank God! It all happened according to the plan.

On the proposed day, I and Bibi took a bus to Curepipe. Goldie would be waiting for us at the stand. After reaching there, we thanked Bibi for lending her hand unconditionally. She left us there in a pool of silence. It was Goldie who broke the ice by asking jovially whether we had been waiting for a long time or we had lengthy conversations without realising. On that day only, I opened up whatever I had in store for him my heart. I told him that I am confused at whether it was my love for him or it was just rebound due to the fact I was dumped lately. The reason behind saying this was that I didn't want to break his heart by cheating on him. As I had to reach home at a fixed time, we took the bus to go back home. Though we sat together, all the way I went on panicking that someone might see us and inform my parents. Luckily, nothing of that sort happened that day.

The excitement of love life had just begun. It was fun spending time together, to go to work early, to have lunches without letting others notice us! After all, as I had already mentioned, the culture was different at that time, and love marriages were rarely witnessed.

Our second date was on a Wednesday. The date was 12th September, 1973. We decided to play a trick on our colleagues so that they don't doubt anything. I took leave for a couple of days whereas he just a half day. Our co-workers were being devoid of any scope to doubt due to this. On the very first of my leave I gave the excuse to my mom that I was not feeling well. The next day, I asked her to allow me to visit the place of the grandma of my cousin, Minta. She was quite reluctant but after much coaxing let me go and asked me to be back by 5pm before my father came back from his workplace.

We planned to meet at the Cosmos Shopping Mall at Curepipe. On reaching there, we spotted Goldie standing in an orange shirt, mustard coloured trouser and his lunch bag. I was quite embarrassed to see the condition of my boyfriend but I didn't grudge as I didn't want to hurt his feelings. He informed us that the three of us would be watching two Indian blockbusters, namely "daag" and "farz" at the Pathe Place Cinema Hall. We settled on that but told him we have to return home at a fixed time.

He went inside for buying the tickets. Inside the hall, I sat in the middle. The more I was looking at him, the stronger became my feelings and he kept on asking when Minta would be leaving. As soon as Minta left, he held my hand and planted a kiss on my lips. I was at a time being nervous, shocked and overjoyed. It was my first time! I din't know how to react and was behaving shyly like a teenager. He held me by my waist and asked me to get closer to him. As it was already 5pm, we took a bus to home and I didn't utter even a single word the whole way. I was in a trance state as well as I was feeling ashamed of what we had done. It was a mixed feeling and I could neither look straight nor talk to him due to sheer shyness. I missed going to work next day too.

So the next day when I went for work was a Friday. When I went inside, I saw him already waiting and he wished me good morning. I wished him too and went straight to my desk. My girlie shyness was following me till then and I was ashamed to talk to him. When he asked why I was maintaining such a distance with him, I told him to which he explained to me that these things were quite natural in love life and there is nothing wrong in this. 12th of September, 1973 was a landmark in my life as on that very day, the light of realisation dawned upon me that I was truly in deep love with Goldie and if ever she had to get into relationship with any person, it's Goldie and Goldie!

Our love, by that time had got to be a routine which we both loved to follow by having and sharing lunches together and writing long love letters for expressing our heartfelt feelings.

It was the month of January, 1974. I had just turned 20 last month. On that day, I asked my mom whether I could pay a visit to my sick friend who was admitted in a hospital after my work was over. This was actually an alibi for going on a date with Goldie at Curepipe. We decided to window shop that day. But God had something else in his mind for me. Coincidentally, I spotted my mom and sister at the shopping mall and froze with fear.

Goldie didn't notice that I had stopped my pace and was talking to my mom. He turned around after a while only to be shocked to see me with my mom and sister. My mom was quite angry at me and ordered me to go home right way. I went to Goldie and delivered her speech to him. So, without a single talk we took a bus and went back home and I gave myself straight away to the bed. After my mom returned, she asked my siblings whether I was back. She called me at dinnertime but I avoided her by saying that I was lacking of appetite.

After dinner that night, she came into my room, sat on my bed and uttered my cherished words. She said that if Goldie really loved me, I should ask him to come at our house and ask my parents for my hand!

CHAPTER-3:
The Marriage With My Love

The relief that mum's words had showered upon me was inexpressible. I couldn't wait to tell Goldie what my mum had just said. That Sunday, a close friend of mine visited me in the afternoon. I told her about my feelings for Goldie, and what my mum thought about it. She had a big smile on her face and assured me that if Goldie really loved me, he would definitely come to my parents with a marriage proposal. "Indeed he loves me", I said to myself and could hardly stop grinning. The next morning I was back at work, and as usual, met Goldie. He had put on a tense face since he feared that my parents, after having come to know about our affair, had turned against it. He seemed rather surprised to notice that I was happier than usual. "What happened to you? I thought you would be tensed after what happened on Saturday" he said. I couldn't stop laughing and told him not to worry. Then we sat down and I conveyed to him my mum's message. He looked happy but I could tell he was nervous inside. "I think it is better to go with my dad. But he won't be free in two months. So, I shall be going next week with my elder cousin." I nodded in agreement and was relieved from inside. Victory was finally in sight!

Goldie and his cousin arrived on Tuesday, 12th March. My dad was unaware of their purpose of visit. He welcomed them into the house assuming they were from my mum's side of the family. "Pearl knows we are coming" explained Goldie. My dad was quite surprised at this—he had never seen the two of them before. He called me to confirm if I really knew about their visit. I was blushing red and just managed to say "yes" in response

15

and left. My dad was puzzled for a moment. The two guests went about explaining their purpose of visit. Now the cloud had cleared. He said to them "I can't say anything at this very moment, bring your parents and we'll talk."

The moment they left, dad came into my room and expressed his disapproval about what had just happened. He said "I give you two choices; either you go to England with your sister and settle there, or you get married and stay here." I didn't think twice—I was too deeply in love to give it a second thought. "I shall marry Goldie" was my prompt reply. "So be it" said my dad with a sigh and explained that the two of us should not meet or spend time together until the two families met. Though I was just 20 at that time, I could hardly wait.

The wait was a quite long one. It wasn't before another six months' time that Goldie's parents finally confirmed their visit. It was a Sunday; the weather was bright and preparations were in full flow in my house to welcome the guests. My family was busy cleaning the entire house, and preparing sweets. It was a tradition in our community to serve guests coming with a marriage proposal with sweets and tea.

The guests arrived. Goldie's parents told mine that he was only 19 years old and he desperately wanted to get the job of a police officer. It was then that I came to know the real age of my man for the first time. His parents further informed that in order to be eligible for his dream job, Goldie needed to be at least 26 years old and unmarried at the same time. The two families converged on the decision that they would wait for another 5 years till his job was finalized and then would get them married in accordance with all religious rituals.

After a successful round of talks, my would-be mother in law wished to have a word with me. I wondered what that was about. She made me sit by her and explained in quiet yet strong words that it was completely unacceptable to have sex before marriage. If we didn't listen to her, and things went wrong, it would be my loss since none else would agree to accept me in marriage. I nodded in agreement, rather scared at her tone. However, I was matured enough to realize that this was a huge responsibility for me and I couldn't do otherwise. At home, I was told that till I was married, I could not be seen with Goldie. However, my parents said that they would allow him to come to our house once every month thinking that by that time we would get to know each other pretty well.

Meanwhile, I and Goldie carried on with our work as usual. Whenever we met, we would talk about our love, and plan our future bit by bit. He was still helping his parents financially with the house loans which meant that he could not afford his own house yet. We gave this some thought and came up with the idea that we would add a few more rooms to his parents' house for ourselves. My sister's husband was a builder by profession and he agreed to carry out this task for free. Time continued to fly and things were starting to fall in place all by themselves. It seemed to be a brief while before finally the wedding date was fixed.

In our culture, it was a custom to get the horoscopes of the bride and the groom matched by a priest to check their marital compatibility. Likewise, our horoscopes were presented to the priest. He was horrified to see that we were both Leos and declared that if we married each other, we would split up in no more than 10 years. The families became concerned; both our families announced their reluctance with our marriage. The glow of happiness in my eyes had transformed to a gloomy cloud in a matter of moments. I wept heavily and even shouted at my dad for pursuing me not to go forward with the marriage. I told him that I loved Goldie more than anything else in this world. Both of us were adamant with our decision—we declared to our families that we loved each other, could not even consider living without each other and so wanted to get married. Ultimately, they relented, though not happy with a marriage against their religious views. They cautioned that the two of us would be responsible if things did not work out in our marriage.

Finally, the wedding date was fixed to be the 9th of April, 1978. Meanwhile, I was noticing changes in Goldie. He had grown possessive over the years. He would not let me talk to any of my other male colleagues and always tried to control my actions. I did not like his attitude and we ended up having heated arguments every day. When the tempers would cool down, Goldie would explain to me that arguments were just the manifestation of a relationship of true love. I would feel sorry when we finally made up, thinking that maybe I was the one over reacting, and maybe I had misunderstood his true feelings. My love for him was too strong to make me think otherwise.

Our culture demanded that we invite all our neighbours, friends and relatives to our weddings. The marital rituals would last for 5 days during which feasts had to be arranged for the visitors every day. Our house was not large enough to accommodate so many people, so we had to build a tent outside. People from both sides were putting in their efforts to help us arrange the marriage.

Six days before my marriage, on the 3rd of April, I was amidst my colleagues for the last time. All of them were wishing me good bye and good luck for my future. As a token of appreciation, my supervisor kissed me on my cheeks and wished me best of luck. Goldie saw that and as had become his habit, became jealous of him. Soon after he accompanied me to our house silently, very upset, and in a sudden fit of rage, shook the tent trying to break it. My dad was close behind and he saw Goldie in the act. He was shocked at the extent of Goldie's anger and warned me that Goldie could never be a good husband. He suggested that I should rethink my decision to marry him since I still had time to change my decision. I answered saying "Don't misjudge him, please. He is a good person inside and I know I'll be very happy with him my whole life." My love for him had made me blind.

The day of the wedding presented new difficulties. In our religion, the priest decided what would be the auspicious time for families to leave the house and also for the wedding. Unfortunately, there was a flood on that very day. We were 2 hours late. I could see that most members of Goldie's family were not happy with the inauspicious start. Finally the wedding was over. After all the religious rituals and the special dinner arranged for all of us, I was extremely tired. I asked Goldie permission to go to bed immediately to which he agreed. We did not have our honeymoon on the night of our wedding.

The next morning we went back to my parents' place for lunch as a part of the tradition. We, as the couple, were presented with lots of sweets, gifts and money as blessings for our new life. When all of this was over, Goldie's cousin helped me tidy up the house. She was really helpful, lending me a hand in arranging our new bed sheets and sorting out my clothes as well. The room which was made ready for us was empty except for the bed and a chair. It was a rather simple arrangement, without any fancy decorations for our honeymoon. But love needs nothing materialistic to flourish; emotions are all that matter. We had the most wonderful night of our lives! The vaccum in the room was filled with our love, happiness and the sweet fruit of our patience of so many years. The night was extremely emotional, full of tears and promises of love made to each other. The next morning, I felt so fresh and grown up; it was as if I had shed my earlier self to evolve into this new Pearl whose world revolved around her husband.

At 8am, Goldie's cousin came in to inform us that breakfast was ready. The two of us took our baths and went for breakfast.

This would be the final feast of the wedding, as all guests were gearing up to leave. The aura of the wedding had gradually started to vanish, and reality started to sink in. Goldie siblings consisted of 3 sisters and 3 brothers. His eldest sister was aged 13, while the other two were 11 year old twins. They were too young for any household chores and it was made clear to me that I had to take up the responsibility now.

My in-laws told me that I was supposed to get down on my knees and polish the floor. The house consisted of 3 bedrooms, a living room, a dining room, a long corridor, kitchen, toilet and bathrooms. The cleaning up took me a lot of time and I could finish only at around 2 pm. My mother in law told me to have a shower and come for lunch. So I did. The entire family sat together and all of us had lunch. I hardly said a word and back into my bedroom as soon as I could. I stood near the window, contemplating about my life—what it was and what it had become. Tears rolled down my cheek and touched the floor.

Goldie noticed me crying. He came up and asked me what was wrong. I reminded him of the promise he had made the last night. He had said that he would not let me miss my family; that he would give me all the attention and love that I needed. I complained that he hadn't come to see me or talk to me all day; the promise had been betrayed. He acted with a lot of compassion and explained to me that his parents did not want him to be "a slave to his wife". I was touched by his words so much that my tears dried up almost immediately. I promised to myself that I would never complain about such an issue anymore since it hurt my feelings badly when my husband was upset.

We were supposed to resume work within a week of the wedding. During the weekends, Goldie's parents called the two of us and explained that after work each day we should come home as early as possible. I would have to prepare dinner for the entire family since my mother in law was giving sewing lessons to some girls from 1pm to 4pm and beyond that, she would have her own sewing orders to work on. They also informed us that I would have to find time to do the ironing as well. It was a wee bit of a relief when I heard that Goldie's eldest sister would be allowed to help me with the cooking somewhat by cutting vegetables and cleaning the kitchen. I was new to the family, and as a newly wedded bride, I was supposed to obey all order of my in-laws. I agreed without hesitation. The next morning, I had to wake up at 5:30am, clean the house, and get ready before 7am so that I didn't fail the deadline of 7:15am in reaching the factory.

My first day at work post marriage was rather dull and ordinary. I met my friends and all of them were talking about how much the marriage had changed me. They said I was not childish anymore, and looked as mature as a married woman should be. It was a busy working day, time flew like it had 4 wings, and very soon the day was over. We finished our work at 5:15 pm and reached home by 5:40. Upon reaching home, I prepared Goldie a cup of tea. After having that, he left without saying anything. This continued day after day—he would leave almost as soon as he reached home. I had no right to ask where he was going, especially not in front of his parents. When we got some time to just the two of us, he would tell me.

My married life had started to become increasingly difficult. I had to cook every day for the family of ten. Rice is the staple diet in Mauritius; I had start with the rice and then prepare the vegetables or meat. Everything had to be in time—the food had to be ready before 7:30pm. At that time, there were no ovens—one had to cook on something that looked rather like a bonfire, with wood burning slowly in between some rocks. The wood had to be put on fire well, which was the difficult task. Once that was done, the cooking would catch pace. We didn't have a washing machine to wash the linen. I had to wash the dirty clothes on a big rock with buckets of water. After an entire day of such household chores, I would go into the house, have a shower, have dinner at 8:30 pm, do the washing and cleaning up, and only then did I have the permission to call it a day. Goldie would be missing as usual, never showing up before 10pm. He would have his dinner on his own and recline to bed. If I bothered to ask where he had been, he would casually reply that his friend owned a theatre and had invited him for a movie. I was never happy with his indifference towards me; however, I was in the process of getting used to it.

They next day after work, I was feeling exhausted as I was not used to so much work. On our way home, Goldie told me that he was going to watch two movies that night so he would come home later than usual. He told me to get one of his sisters to sleep next to me. He would go and sleep in his brothers' room. I hardly had a chance to say anything since we had already reached home. As the night was drawing up on me, I was finding it impossible to sleep; I was perplexed and angry and could not find a reason why my husband would choose to leave me alone at night when we had been married just for a few days. I could hear his motorbike at 12:30 am. The next morning, when he came to see me, I was up and in front of the mirror, getting ready for work. He asked me how I was. I was too angry with him to reply. He waited for a moment and then said "I'm talking to you". I kept myself quiet. He came in closer, slapped me in a fit of rage, and left. My tears knew no bounds. I had never expected my love to slap me like this. My pride had been shattered. He didn't even bother to come and see me. When it was time for us to leave for work, he simply sent his sister to tell that he was waiting outside for her. I didn't even have my breakfast and left.

When we got back home after work, I heard Goldie asking his mum where his dad's newspapers were. He wasn't going to go out and so he needed those to keep himself busy. I carried on with my chores the usual way. At my in-laws' place, we never had a proper family dinner. One would eat only when he was hungry. When I went for dinner after shower, I saw Goldie having dinner in front of the TV. I went into the kitchen—his mother was serving dinner to the kids, so she served me too. I had a nice time chatting with my sisters in law and having dinner. When it was over, I went back into the room as usual. Not much later, Goldie came in as well. He apologised and told me that he loved me very much. He added that he could not bear the fact that I was not talking to him. I explained to him why I had acted that way in the morning. According to me, it was unfair—I had left my parents, brothers and sisters to come to his place. I didn't think that I would have to sleep alone only after a few days of my marriage. He dealt the matter with compassion and promised not to go and watch movies till late again. He promised me that he would be there with me every night. He said he loved me; he wanted to make me happy and wanted me to lead a happy life. As from that night, he stopped going to the movies till really late, but he always went out.

There was no phone at my in laws' place. I could never talk to my family even if I wanted to. I told Goldie that I wished to go and visit my family. He said he would take me there on the following Sunday. I still had my eldest sister working in the same factory as mine; still I missed everyone else. As promised, we went to visit my parents on the Sunday and spent a few hours there. I felt extremely happy; however, deep inside, I was sad, thinking about how happy I used to be in my parents' house. I had the notion that being married only meant being loved and living a wonderful life. But my days after marriage had taught me otherwise. None could ever replace the love one gets from her parents. When it was time for me to leave, I was in tears once again. I told my parents that I would visit them more often. It was ironical that I had to crave so much to meet them while they lived just 2 miles away.

CHAPTER-4:
A Changed Feeling

As time was flying away, I could feel as well as notice a change in my married life. Goldie was no longer his earlier self. There was a crack in our love. Goldie didn't care for me that much anymore and worst of all, he wasn't a bit responsible. The other members of Goldie's family used to keep me aloof of everything. They didn't bother to make me feel like their daughter and I could not even consider myself to be a full member of their family.

Even after seven months had passed after our marriage, my husband's luggage and belongings were still in his younger brother's room. It was a practice for me to witness him every morning getting up in our bedroom and hurrying towards his sibling's house for getting ready. One day, I dared to ask him to bring his belongings and keep those in our house. In turn, he asked me to take his mom's permission for doing that instead of taking any action himself. The very next morning, I, maintaining all possible courtesy asked my mother-in-law very politely if I could shift my husband's belongings to our own house to which she started wailing and accused me of taking their son away from them! After that she permitted to do that by bit by bit so that it was easier for her to bear with the fact. I agreed with her and told her that I would let her know the time I would start. I deciphered the entire conversation to my husband to which he replied back that I must give his mom some time before shifting his things.

Finally I and my husband came to a settlement that on every Wednesday and Saturday, while I would be busy in doing the ironwork from 8:30 p.m. till midnight, he would go to his friend's theatre for watching movies and return late at night.

Time was flying away very quickly. Christmas and New Year were knocking at the door. The marriage of one of my cousins was fixed on 26th of January in the year of 1979. The day fixed turned out to be a weekday and the time given was 4 pm so Goldie said that he would not be able to go there because of his work. Goldie asked me to tell my brother to pick me up and drop me back to home after the function got over. I settled down with that but afterwards I don't know why he changed his mind and told me that he would leave me at my parental house in the morning when he goes for work.

He accomplished that the next day and when I reached my mom's place I saw that my sisters were quite busy getting ready. I also started with them and in the meantime, one of my sisters took notice of my ear-rings and liked them very much. She asked if we can exchange as that would be going well along with our dresses. I agreed and finally after we all were ready, we set out for the community hall where the marriage ceremony was taking place. It was about 6-7 miles away from our house. After the wedding, we all went to our cousin's place for reception.

As it was getting dark and late, I asked my brother to drop me home but he turned down because he had some other work to do. In the meantime, somebody came and informed me that Goldie had been waiting for me at my mom's place. I hurriedly reached there and was worried to see him upset and restless. Without a single talk, we got on his bike and set out for our home. Even after reaching home we kept mum and had our dinner in pin drop silence and went to bed as we both were upset.

Renooka Gopaul

Next morning when I was getting ready for work, Goldie came and noticed the changed ear rings and asked in a doubtful tone whose they were. I was so grieved by his doubtfulness that out of frustration I replied that I didn't know whom those belonged to. At this, he got extremely furious and snatched away the ear rings from my ears harshly. I was in lot of pain and started shedding tears and said that I would not be able to go to work in this sorry state of mind as well as body. Things got worse at this when he brought the drinking can meant for dogs and started hitting me with that. Blood was oozing out from my head and I was in unbearable pain.

My mother-in-law turned up for handling the situation and took me to the hospital for making things easier. The doctor had to give me 7 stiches on my head and I had to get a big plaster as well. He asked me what happened but I simply lied saying that I fell down accidentally and got the injury. But he was no fool and he could easily make out what could have happened as I had been crying for a long time. My mother-in-law was a bit kind to me and out of sympathy she asked to stay overnight at their place. Later that day when Goldie came back home, he didn't even bothered to ask about my health or condition or where I was. He just went inside to sleep in our room in quite a tranquil state of mind.

The next morning I was completely aware that my life had changed drastically and converted into a woeful one indeed. When I went to my workplace next Monday, all my colleagues were shocked to see my condition and kept on asking the reason. The only thing I could do was to give a fake smile and lie flawlessly that it was all because of the concrete edge of the staircase where I fell and hurt myself. After getting back home, Goldie started conversing with me rather making it obligatory without a tone apology or even a bit of regret in his voice. I was made to feel that I was the one who was guilty.

My sister who worked along with me in the same factory must have told my parents about all these and that evening at 6p.m. they came to pay a visit to me. My younger brother-in-law went to a friend's place to inform him about the visit of his in-laws so that he returned home that very moment. He came back and my parents asked him the reason behind all these things. He told them flatly the entire truth and grudged about going to my parent's house often. He without caring how one would feel said that he just don't like that. My parents were quite displeased at his cold and bad behaviour and dropped in angrily that in that case they were not ready to leave their daughter with such a person. The only thing Goldie did was that he turned around and said in a dominating tone that I if I wished to leave, he would not stop me. But If I chose to stay with him, his wished me to be a housewife and leave work and I had to obey him.

In a flash, I remembered my parents saying before my marriage that if I chose to marry Goldie they would not be helping me at any cost. My self-respect did hurt me at that time and I said to my parents that as I was married now and had my own husband, household to look after, I would be staying there only, whatever be the conditions therein.

As a girl, I knew that once a girl gets married she becomes just a guest at her father's house. So, she would not leave her husband's home at any cost and she would do that only when she dies. At least in our culture, in those days it was the common belief. So, I thanked my parents for their kindness and sympathy they had shown and they left my house in tears. Later on that night I and my husband had a serious talk and God was kind enough to bestow the realisation on Goldie that I loved him from the core of my heart. He also said he loved me very much and from then onwards, he would not be violent with me anymore and take care of me and reciprocate my love properly. He promised me a healthy married life and a world where there would be only he and me.

I continued to be grief stricken that whole week and I was also getting bored at home because of not going to work. But I didn't dare to grudge as I was quite scared of losing Goldie. A fear always haunted me that he would leave me if I disobey him. Alas! What a fool I was! I didn't know what true love was. I was mad after the superficial love that Goldie had for me but I realised these facts long after when my life had already been turned into hell.

Anyways, in that weekend without informing me anything, Goldie went to his mom's place and brought all his belongings. In half an hour only, everything was set right. I was quite happy thing that we were getting closer. On Sunday afternoon, when Goldie was lazing out on bed, I went to talk to him about a serious matter. I tried to explain to him that it was getting hard to get through the expenses of our daily life as a major part of his salary was going straight to his father's hand and he was having just 100 bucks as his pocket money. Though we didn't require paying any bills still we had to pay for the furniture which we had bought in instalments. So, I pleaded with him to let me go to work again for making all the ends meet. At last, he agreed on one condition that I would not tell anyone about all the happenings, not even to my parents. I settled on that and returned to my work again in the beginning of February, 1979.

I was again getting back to good old jovial self by seeing that we were coming closer. He seemed to be more loving and caring than before. Simultaneously, he was also worried about his goal of becoming a policeman because he was already 24 years old by then and he had to start job by 26 years maximum. So, it became almost a routine for him to apply for a job whenever and wherever he found a vacancy.

It was 10th of September, 1979 when Goldie received the first call for interview for the post of a fireman. He started his job as a fireman by the end of that month and his first posting was at the airport where his team had been working. After two months, he received a call letter from the police department for measurements. He underwent all the medical tests and finally, he was selected as a trainee police officer that year only. He was so overjoyed that he was no longer in any mood to continue his work as a fireman at the airport.

So, for the next one week he decided to accompany me to my workplace before leaving for training and pick me up after my work was over. We used to walk that much way as it was only at a distance of 15-20 minutes. We used to enjoy the walk together very much as if time had come to a stop and it would be lasting for long. It was full of feelings and love for each other.

But my days of happiness came to an end rather early. Goldie started his police duty on the 10th of December, 1979. Goldie came and informed me that the training in the next 6 months was going to be much tougher and it was required for him to stay at the police barrack for all week days. The barrack was about half an hour walking distance from our house. For that reason he would not be able to come to home on weekdays so he would be coming on Saturday afternoons and returning on Mondays. He also said that he would me missing me very much for not seeing me for 5 days as it was the first time since 1973 we would not be staying away from each other. I too was much grieved after hearing that but I decided to be strong and consoled my husband by saying that I would be paying a visit to him on the very first of his life at the barracks.

It was the 16th of December and Goldie's first day at the barrack. He accompanied me at my workplace. There he gave me a goodbye kiss and left the place with a heavy heart. After the day's work was over, when I was returning home, I could feel the extreme loneliness. I was in the habit of having him by my side every day and from that day he would not be there. I was grieved at this thought and hurried home but could not get any relief as the house seemed empty and I was sinking into it. After cooking dinner for the family, I went to my room and started crying bitterly. After wiping my tears I looked at the clock and saw it was already 8 pm. But as it was summer season, I went to my mother-in-law to ask for her permission to visit Goldie at the barracks. She was quite delighted and expressed the desire to accompany me.

So, I, my mother-in-law, my twin sister-in-laws and my younger brother-in-law set out to visit Goldie. When we reached there, he was filled with extreme joy on seeing us. He greeted me with a kiss and hugged me saying that he loved me umpteenth number of times. He also said that he missed me a lot. After few minutes somebody came and told us that meeting time was over. So we had to part with a heavy heart and I could saw that tears were rolling down his cheeks and he gave me a hug and all that he could utter was "See you soon".

The next day we paid a visit to Goldie was a Wednesday. He looked happier than before and had started talking like trainee police officer. I was quite relieved and happy to see him recovering from the grief and concentrating on his work. We came back home and I asked one of my sister-in-laws to sleep with me that whole week. I was waiting eagerly for Saturday to come as Goldie would be back on that day. He was supposed to reach at 9 am. I was so happy to see him at the gate at 8:45p.m. He met and gave me a hug at first, and then he went to meet his parents and other members of the family. He spent some time with them, gossiped and then came back to me and asked me to save a few hours for just two of us.

I was very happy to hear this and completed all my household chores as fast as possible and rushed to our bedroom to join Goldie for watching T.V. We spent a few hours very close to each other and talking about love. It was the first time after my marriage we were being so intimate and I was the happiest wife that day. I felt that it was the staying apart from each other which had worked magic. Goldie after this distance had been able to realise how much he loved and cared for me. That night he told me that wanted to go out for a movie and needless to say, he would not be back before morning. I didn't complain as I was just happy with the thought that he was back home and near to me. He made me feel that he was proper, caring and a true loving husband.

Soon, the lovely weekend came to an end and Goldie was prepared to leave on Monday morning. I was sad and could not wait for another weekend to come when Goldie would be coming again. Next weekend also he did come but I could notice as well as feel a change in his routine. During their training session they had to give exams and thus prepare for them so he was busy with his studies and could make out very little time to spend with me. I realised that it was not possible for Goldie to concentrate on our married life thoroughly. I made my heart strong and made it understood by saying to myself that I must make sacrifices otherwise it they can't be rewarded back with good things.

One night Goldie called me and enquired if even then I loved him or had started feeling that he was a boring nerd who was always busy with his books and had no time for me.

I replied back in positive that I loved him till then and most probably, even more than before. These days of staying alone had made me feel that I loved him more and if he did not believe he could ask his heart and I could be sure that it would give the same answer because I knew he too loved me the same.

At this, Goldie was very pleased and he said smilingly that he did love me from the core of his heart and more than his life.

Though I used to stay alone for 5 days each week, he would never allow me to go to my parental home often. He told that whenever I should go there, he would accompany me. In the first weekend of February of the year 1980, I asked him to take me to mom's house but he simply denied promising that he would take me in the next weekend surely.

On Monday morning, when he was ready to go back, he told me that as coming Thursday was going to be a public holiday, he would return home by Wednesday night. I was quite happy. The public holiday was for observing Maha Shivaratri. In Mauritius people of our culture go to a sacred lake situated in the south which was known as "Ganga Talao". We had to go there on foot and brought back some water from that lake which is given to Lord Shiva in the temple as an offering. After Goldie was back that afternoon, we all set out for the lake. The entire from our home to the lake and back to home on foot used to took 5 long hours. When we reached there, one of the neighbours of my parents informed me that my dad fell down and it was suspected that it might be a stroke so he had been admitted to a hospital and I must pay a visit to him.

I was totally devastated and scared and wanted to go to my parent's house right away. On our way back Goldie was quite upset with that and told me I was being very stupid because I was crying and the neighbour did not do the right thing by informing me about my dad's illness. When we reached home, it was almost 4:30 am. Everyone else in our house went to sleep but I started doing my household chores as usual and wanted to complete them as soon as possible. This was because we were required to go to the temple early next morning and after coming back from the temple, I wanted to go straight to my parent's home to see my dad.

Next morning, Goldie woke up late as usual which upset me even more. From the temple, we came back home straight and

I pleaded with Goldie to take me to my mom's place but to my shock, he just shouted at me refusing to take me there. I was so grief-stricken that without finding another way, I sat outside and started crying. In the meantime, my father-in-law came on to the spot and enquired about the entire matter. When I told him he asked my husband to drop me at my mom's place. He reluctantly gave me a lift and after dropping me on the road in front of my mom's place told me that I should ask my brother to take me to hospital and he would pick me up in the evening from home.

When I entered the house, the atmosphere was awkwardly silent. Lots of relatives and friends had come to support my mom in this bad time. They were quite anxious about my father's adverse condition of health. They asked me if I wanted to pay a visit to the hospital. I nodded in affirmative and they took me to the hospital. I was shocked to see my father in state of coma lying motionlessly for the first time in my life. I somehow managed to control my tears and went to talk to the nurse in charge. She told me that my father suffered a severe cerebral attack and haemorrhage was there and he would not survive. I came back speechless but could not tell anything to my mom. However, I took two of my sisters into confidence. In the evening Goldie came to take me back and consoled my mom and said that he would pay a visit to my dad in the evening as that was the visiting time.

Even after coming back home, I remained quite upset and could hardly eat or sleep. I could not express what I was feeling. My head was feeling tizzy. It seemed to be going round and round. Next morning when I woke up, I was in no mood to go to work. So, I asked Goldie to drop me at my mom's place but he turned down my proposal saying that we would be visiting dad in the evening. I had to go to work at 7:30 am and it was 9:10 am when I was summoned to the office. There I saw my brother waiting for me and from his unusual and restless behaviour I could predict that something was wrong. He asked me to go with him immediately as dad was seriously ill. Later on, on the way he broke the news that dad was no more. I did not know how to react as I was totally shocked. My brother told me to think of a way so that this devastating news could be deciphered to my mom. He dropped me home and went back to the hospital for collecting the dead body and death certificate. I did not know how to tell mom and I just remember that my sister started weeping bitterly on hearing that and my mom just rushed outside to know about her husband when our neighbour informed her.

I missed my dad like hell. It was hard for me to accept the truth that he was no more. I told my husband that loss of my dad had created a deep emptiness in my life and it was only he who could fulfil that gap by being affectionate and caring. He promised to be more loving and caring from that day onwards.

It was already the month of June and Goldie's training came to an end. After the training and exams were over, Goldie secured the 3rd position in the whole group and he got a few days leave before joining for work permanently in the dog-training section. His work was on alternate days because he had to work for 24 hours and he would get 24 hours leave after that. So, the situation was like that he would spend a night at workplace and another at home.

After two years of our marriage, Goldie's mom expressed her desire to have a grandchild which Goldie supported. He came to me and said that we must start consult a specialist and start treatment. For that, we need to save a lot as the treatment would cost much. We went to a doctor and had all the tests done but it gave no fruitful result. So, I decide to go for a check-up abroad. I also started to save and Goldie went to his dad to let him know that he could no longer be able to hand over his wages to him but he would pay some of the bills. My father-in-law agreed to that.

We started saving but I could notice some negative changes in my husband. He had started maintaining distance with me. My sixth sense told me that he was cheating on my back but I didn't want to pay much heed to my intuitions as I was till then madly in love with Goldie and I prayed to God that all my doubts turn out to be false.

CHAPTER-5:

Love That Hurt

By the mid of year 1981, we decided to start my treatment abroad. We had grown desperate for a child. According to the terms of his service, Goldie was not allowed any leave till 3 years were over. I would have to be on my own on my journey to Germany and Switzerland. I started out alone in the quest of fertility. I consulted three different doctors, but none of them succeeded. Finally, I ended up in France where a lady doctor gave me some hope; however the cost of treatment would be very high. I didn't know where from to arrange such a large amount; I was at a dead end. After a lot of introspection, I weighed my options and decided I had none. There was no way I would go back without completing my treatment. I decided to make myself strong and stay back; I would put all my energy towards earning the necessary amount.

I applied for a visa and was allowed a years' time. I tried hard and managed to get employed as a live-in nanny for a four year old boy. I had to teach him as well as look after him. The wages were 2500 Francs per month. I loved my job; children had always attracted me, perhaps the lack of one of my own had aggravated my emotions. However, the lady had not paid me for my services for nine and half months. Her excuse would be that she was in the process of getting her divorce and she would pay me as soon as she received alimony from her rich husband. I did not object considering her difficulties, although not happy with the delay. My husband had completed 3 years of his service by that time and he was free to take leave. He obtained a visiting visa and came to France to see me. On reaching my working place, he asked the lady for my wages since it had been a long time without any payment. The excuse was repeated and we waited rather reluctantly. But the lady turned out to be a fraud; by the end of that week she had disappeared leaving the little boy with her grandma, while the house was sold by her husband.

I had never felt so betrayed in my life. I had given it everything I had with the hope that I would be able to go back home with the assurance of becoming a mother. The dream had been shattered. We had nowhere to stay, not even enough money. A 3 years visa was all we could bank on. We decided to fly back to England and find out a way to revive ourselves. Since me and Goldie didn't have a civil marriage back home, the authorities didn't recognize Goldie as my husband. We decided to have a civil marriage in England, however, not before consulting a doctor once more. The fees were a hefty £40 but all the doctor did was to check my stomach, find a scar on it and ask for my health reports from Mauritius. I had received the scar a long 12 years back, and as I contacted the doctors in Mauritius, I learnt that they had no records of mine. The visit to the doctor had once again turned out to be futile.

We had a civil marriage in England on the 23rd of August 1983, in the Enfield registrar. Following the marriage, we booked a return ticket and flew back to Mauritius on the 30th of December. I had already realised that going back home would mean a life devoid of any job, whereas staying back would present me with a lot of opportunities even though I was already 30 years old. The laws said that I could apply for the visa as soon as I got a job. Although I was making a huge sacrifice with my career, I considered what I would gain—my love, my heart, my joy, my world—my dear husband. The balance tilted over to the latter and I didn't hesitate to return. I desperately hoped that the New Year would turn things around and make me happier; hope was all I could do.

The year 1984 was going to be arguably the most decisive year of my entire life. Now that I had returned home, and had no job to fall back on, I was entirely dependent on my husband. Both financially and emotionally, he had to be my lifeline. I felt it would be hard for the two of us to survive without my job. Goldie assured me his wages would be enough. He promised me love and fidelity. He said "I love you; you are my wife in front of God and by law. I will look after you till your death. I won't feel bad that you can't give me a child. I love you; I don't want to lose you. You will always be the only candle that will always burn in the cathedral of my heart. Trust me I won't cheat on you." The words brought tears in my eyes. Every time he promised to love me forever, I would embrace him tighter, hoping that he would never let our bond weaken.

Days came and went and soon it was February. One day, as I was tidying up Goldie's wardrobe, my eyes happened to chance on a little box. I opened it and to my utter shock I found that it was full of love letters from different women I never knew about. The cloud slowly cleared from my mind as I was halfway through the first letter. I realised that the same person who would promise to be loyal to me, had been cheating on me all along. Tears rolled down my eyes; the grief of knowing that my husband was seeing other women had started to burn me from inside.

When Goldie returned, I confronted him about the letters. He seemed to be at a loss for words initially; but he pulled himself together and said that while I was abroad fighting my fortunes, lots of women were writing such letters to him. I knew that would be impossible since there was no way they would have known his address without him giving it to them. I knew he was lying through his teeth, but I calmed myself down thinking it was too late already. He tried to convince me by saying that he had never replied to any of those letters. He continued his ramblings saying that even though I was not able to give him a child, he would never have another woman in his life. He promised to prove his love for me.

My jobless days had left me bored and dull. I asked Goldie to finish building the kitchen so that we could have one of our own. He took no less than 2 years to get it completed finally. Meanwhile, I could sense my husband changing for the worse. He used to be irritated at all times, always screaming at me for even trivial matters. He had resumed his earlier practice of coming home late at night. I had the feeling all along that it was the wrong decision to leave England and come back home; nevertheless it was too late now. Deep inside, I knew there was someone else in his life. Recently, he had started beating me up as well, perhaps to tell me by actions rather than words how much he hated me. I had trusted my entire life with him, and he abused that trust. I had nowhere to go, none to fall back on, but only left to myself to cry and pray.

On the 4th of June, Goldie returned home early rather unusually at about 4pm. He told me that there was something serious that he wanted to discuss with me. I jumped into the middle of the bed—sitting in the middle made me feel like a queen. I hoped that he would confess his guilt and say that he was sorry and come back to me. Confess he did—he simply said "You know Pearl, I have a girlfriend."

I laughed about what he had just said and took it like a joke. I told him that if this was true, I would commit suicide. But Goldie had made up his mind to say what he had come to say. He replied "I am not joking. There is really someone in my life. She is 22 years old and is ready to give me a baby." He begged me, saying "You will be my wife forever. And after the birth of the child, I'll bring the child home and leave the girl where she is." The dreaded words had finally being spoken. My eyes swelled up and felt like bursting out with hurt and betrayal.

I told him in a matter of fact tone that what he wanted could not be agreed to. Being a woman myself, I knew what it meant to a woman when his man left her, and I would never let another woman go through that pain knowingly. "If you really love me, you should forget about her and give our marriage another chance" was my answer.

His shroud of love and calmness had vanished. He let go of his I and told me fiercely that he could not live without a child and if that would bother me, I should take a break, go to England for a year and come back only after the birth of the child. I refused straightaway. But he had made up his mind. He said it was his final decision to move on with his new girlfriend and I either had to accept it and stay here or leave for England. My love for him was blind and had never diminished even having suffered such a betrayal. I decided to stay back and desperately hoped that I would be able to persuade him to change his mind. My sister had come to my parents' place on holiday from England. I told him to take me there and let me visit her and I would have a break as well. He agreed.

His indifference towards me and his newfound love in his girlfriend had started to take shape. His confession to me made him think that there was no need to hide facts now. He started taking out his girlfriend with him wherever he went, without bothering about what people would say. Every morning I would wake up early, prepare his breakfast, and iron his clothes for him to go to work. Throughout the day I could only think about Goldie—what he was up to, whether he was with this new girl. I knew that I had chosen to stay back consciously, and as promised, I would have to share my husband with another woman without protesting.

People had started to talk about the new couple. A friend of mine, a French lady, had seen them together and informed me. I could do nothing other than cry, and told her to keep it to herself and not tell me if she saw them again in future. The less I knew the better. My friend was from a different culture and more modern than I was. She suggested that I could ask Goldie to find a surrogate mother. I welcomed the idea, imagining it would solve our problems. But when I shared the idea with him, he refused straightaway, saying he wanted a child with love. My hopes were shattered and I knew instantly that our marriage had come to a dead end. Still I told my friend that perhaps he would change since he knew how much I loved her. Unfortunately, my friend passed away a few months later, leaving me to fight alone against this harsh world. I broke down emotionally.

I was so tempted to leave; but due to some unexplainable reason I continued to hope that my love would succeed, and Goldie would change for the better. Things were only becoming worse, as I felt the distance between us growing with each passing day. I started feeling like a maid, who was just living in the house to do the household chores. I would often get beaten up by a police belt without reason. We never even had a conversation; as if we were two unknown people living under the same roof. I would often cry and ask myself "Who is this man? Is he my love, my world, my husband? Or is he just a scary man whom I had failed to recognize completely?"

From love, my feelings for him had transformed into fear. He was indifferent, hardly noticing what he was doing to me. Our religion told us that a wife should always listen to the husband and obey him whatever his orders. She had no right to answer him back or argue with him. I had learnt to be a pious woman, and had never violated any of these. I would only pray to the Almighty saying "Change my life. Make us happy. Forgive me if I have done anything wrong. Please give me some happiness."

I had become fed up with my life. I decided to worship Goddess "Durga" and started praying and observing fasts. I had heard people say that she is a woman and a mother, and she would understand the pain I was going through. But soon I realized that I was too weak both physically and mentally to carry on with the fasts. I had to stop, and accept my life as it was.

Time was passing very slowly. I decided try talking to Goldie for a final time before calling it quits. I tried to talk to him nicely and make him change his mind. But he had no intentions to change. He said "You are my wife; you will be in my house and in my right arm. She will be out, and in my left arm." All I could say was a weak "Okay". My voice had choked. The next day I was weeping heavily when my brother in law noticed me. He came up to me, tried to calm me down, and told me to stop crying and make a move. He said "I know where my brother goes. One day, I'll take you there, and you try to have a word with that girl." I agreed since this was my last hope.

One Sunday, my brother in law accompanied me to the girl's house. I knocked at the door. A lady came and opened the door, who must have been the girl's mum. She asked me who I was to which I replied that I was her daughter's friend. When I went in, I asked her whether she knew Mr Goldie. The lady answered in the affirmative. Then I told her that I was Goldie's wife. The mother was shocked to learn this. She seemed to have no idea and called her daughter downstairs immediately. I tried to explain to the girl that I loved my husband and would not leave him at any cost. Now the ball was in her court to decide what she wanted to do. She replied "If your husband loved you, I wouldn't be in his life. I came after you. So he loves me, not you. You know that you can't give him a kid, but I will."

I was shocked at the girl's response; I had thought being a girl she would be alarmed knowing Goldie's reality. But she seemed to be supporting him completely. "Okay", I said, "I can challenge you that my husband loves me. If something like this happens in my life, I will come in front of you and you can spit in my face. Thank you and bye!"

That day, when Goldie returned, I spilled the beans to him. I felt he should know the truth about what had happened. He was shocked and furious. "I am going to bring her in this house. You can pack your belongings and go", said he and slapped me on my face. I started screaming and shouting to stop him, terrified that he would really do what he had just uttered. But he left. My father in law came to see me and told me to stay there and wait for Goldie. He returned really late and went straight to bed.

Next Friday onwards, I started observing fasts for Goddess Durga. During the following 16 weeks of fasting, I incessantly prayed to the Goddess to help me—if I had to leave then help me leave happily and if I had to stay then help me stay happily. The 16 weeks passed like 16 days for me, I was so deeply involved in the worship. A few more days later, there was a knock on the door. A friend of Goldie had come to visit us. Goldie welcomed him in. I overheard their discussion. He was asking Goldie if he could borrow me for a few days to take charge of his factory since the man who had been at that job earlier had left without notice. Goldie asked me if I was interested. I had nothing else to do at home other than get sad, so this was really a welcome opportunity for me. I said "yes" and went back into my room. The next day, he sent his driver to pick me up for at 11 am. I was supposed to appear for an interview and then get acquainted with my job.

I went into my new workplace and asked the boss if the formalities could be completed quickly. I knew very well that Goldie wouldn't be happy if I wasn't home before he returned. I couldn't return before 12:30 pm and he was already there having his lunch. As I had feared, he got furious seeing me come home late. He started shouting and picked up a stone to hit me. I ran to save myself and hid behind his dad. The latter stopped Goldie. I was stunned at the way Goldie had reacted. He asked me why I had gone. I reminded him that he had permitted me to go to his friend's factory the previous day and now he couldn't deny it. He was red with rage and took his belt off and started beating me up like an animal. I was screaming with pain. His dad rushed in again and shouted at him. He stopped punishing me and went into the room. Before leaving for work, he dragged me out of the house and said "You go now. I don't want you in my life anymore."

As soon as he left, my father in law told me "It's better if you go back to your mum's place and work. You will be better off than in his hands. You are not my daughter in law, rather you've been like my daughter since the first day you came into the family." I wept in his arms for a moment and felt completely helpless. Then I took courage from his words and made preparations to go back to my parents' place, once and for ever. The trust I had so far harboured in my love had finally been shattered to pieces.

CHAPTER-6:
A Changed Life In England

I went on shedding tears for two hours continuously from 1p.m. to 3p.m. as if my entire soul were forcing me to shed them so that I get rid of the anguish and anger which was buried deep inside my heart. I was feeling much light hearted after that and I finally went to my father-in-law's room for asking his permission to use the phone to call a taxi. When I entered the house of my mom, she and my siblings were totally taken aback acknowledging that I had been beaten up all along. I have never complained to them against Goldie but on that day, they had to witness severe injuries on my arm and back which were bleeding and a swollen wrist. My mom decided to take any step only after my brothers returned. After they came back, they settled down to have a serious talk with me. They asked me whether it was my final decision and confirmed whether I should be going back or not. I said in a stern voice that I had taken that step to move ahead in my life and not for looking backward.

They took me to the hospital to get my wounds treated. I was given three stitches and the doctor also advised me to go for a scan in my head as well as wrist. The only type of medicine given was pain killing tablets. As it was a police case, I had to lodge a complaint against Goldie and was made to fill up a form under the Act 58. A police officer came for enquiry and I gave a statement against Goldie. But afterwards I was in dilemma pondering over whether I did right or wrong. My brain was being logical and telling me that it was right to punish a person like Goldie but my poor heart was still filled with blind love for him. So, I asked the officer if I could have some time to think over the matter and gave the statement next morning. The officer agreed to that and I was happy because according to me, advices are often given by the night time.

The next day when I was talking to my mom regarding this I could find the anxiety on her face. It was the anxiety of a mother mixed with affection for her daughter. She also told me that I was very lucky to have the relatives and friends by my side when I needed them most whereas, on the other hand the person whom I loved and cared for even more than myself didn't have the least botheration for me.

The pain both in my wounds and mind were still afresh. Moreover the anxiety on my mom's face made me understand that what Goldie did was absolutely wrong and I should take revenge. So, I gave the statement against him. According to the law of our land he had committed a grave crime by raising his hands on me. There were other serious offences against him. Firstly, he was not supposed to leave his workplace during lunch hours and secondly, no government property was to be used in any sort of personal matters. The belt with which he used to beat me up was a part of his uniform. So, I came to know that as a punishment, he had to appear before the commissioner of police and admit his crime and would most probably be suspended.

I was given a few days to take my statement back. So, the very next morning he sent his mom, a colleague and brother-in-law to have a talk with me. They pleaded with me to take the statement back but I refused as my mom and brothers wanted me to take revenge and I didn't want to go against their wish as they were the people who supported me during the grave moment of my life. My heart perhaps would have melted for Goldie had he come in person to talk to me. But he was filled up to the brim with his ego and never turned up.

At last, one day, he came to my workplace to have a talk with me regarding that and asked me to do that favour to him. I was moved by his words and we went to the police station on his motor bike for taking the statement back. I was such a fool to think that he had changed for the better and had come to apologise and take me back home. But as soon as his purpose was over, the beast inside him came out. While returning back, he abused me with slangs and even told me that he could get better girls than me and I was of no use to him. My heart broke into pieces hearing all these and all I could do was to rush inside and cry to my heart's content. I could not imagine how he could tell me such nonsense things even after I went against my mom and brothers just because I didn't want to hurt him and see him happy.

It was on the 4th day of April when Goldie sent his youngest brother to me in order to inform that he would be waiting at the shop to meet me. In the afternoon, I said to my sister that I would be going to the shop where we first met. When I reached there, I saw Goldie waiting for me. He had come to give the news that he will be leaving for England shortly afterwards for a training. The 8th of April was a Sunday and on that very day, he left for England without any regret or any arrangement for me.

Life didn't stop for anything and in due course of time I changed my workplace. I started working in another factory and it was the month of January, 1990 when the security of that factory came and informed me that a person had been waiting at the gate to see me. I hastily went there and was surprised as well as overjoyed to see Goldie standing there. It was not easy for him to find out my changed workplace so I thought that he might have understood his fault and had come along to ask me return back. But my happiness didn't last long. He had not come to take me back; rather he turned up to give the so called joyful news that he was going to be fathered by his girlfriend at last. As I was still his legitimate wife, he could not declare his marriage with his girlfriend and as a consequence, the child would also be illegitimate according to the law of Mauritius. So, the main purpose of his visit was to take my permission so that he could declare the coming child as his own. I was so hurt by his intentions that I said I had nothing to say. He was not a person to give up and left by saying that he would turn up again.

On that very day, I learnt from a female colleague in the factory that the girl with whom Goldie had had an affair was her niece and they were married to each other. After coming to know this, I realised how big a fool I was and how big a liar as well as cheater was Goldie. I made up my mind to teach him a lesson next day. On 16th of April, he came and informed me that his girlfriend had given birth to a baby girl and he was very proud to be her father. But he didn't even bother to notice even once the pain on my face. All that he asked for was my permission to declare his daughter. Out of frustration I replied in negative and rushed inside in tears.

I felt like cursing my weak heart which again made me feel sorry for refusing and hurting him even after this big drama of his. I could not accept the fact that I had broken up with him. I still used to get ready to impress him as he was near me. I used to all the things as if we were dwelling together. From the day onwards I had left his house, I stopped worshipping or offering prayers to God as I believed that there was no supernatural power called "God". Had he been there, he would have helped me, guided me and above all, would not have let such a situation to occur in my life.

My life totally changed from that day onwards. I clearly realised that I have lost everything in life. I lost the person whom I loved so deeply. He was my life, and he simply kicked me out of his life. It was hard for me to survive in this way as it seemed to me that I was no one without him and life was meaningless as there was no reason left for me to live. I was also aware of the fact that no one or nothing could be able to replace Goldie in my heart. Though I was extremely hurt, I told myself that I could not forget the ritual, the oaths, the relationship and therefore, he would continue to dwell in my heart.

In the same year on 16th of October, I left Mauritius for going to England, determined to rebuild my life there. After reaching England, I joined a computer course. But, it was not at all easy for me to pay the monthly fees. So, I decided that I must start working in order to earn my livelihood as well as to pay for my education. So, I started working as a cleaner 20 hours per week. At the same time, I went along with my education too. I was allowed to work during the extra hours on the holidays and got extra wages for that. My boss told me that I could also work as a housekeeper for 8 hours per day. It was a great opportunity for me and as I was in utter need of money, I accepted the offer at once. So, I used to work very hard on the weekdays.

On Saturdays and Sundays, I used to be free and on those days, I used to tidy my house and do all other household chores. After finishing all those, I would go to meet my cousin at 11a.m. who used to live nearby and often, we had lunch outside and went for shopping. After coming back home, I would go to my cousin's place for dinner as her husband was working in night shifts and she had two kids. So, we both used to have a good time gossiping, watching T.V., cooking and eating the meals together. As her house was just 5 minutes walking distance from mine, I could easily come back by 9p.m.

On the Sundays, my cousin used to come for lunch. After having our lunch together, either we would go to the park or spend our time taking rest or lazing around. She used to go back to her home by 5p.m. I was very happy to get a relative abroad and very pleased with the thing that she often paid visits to my house. Gradually, in due course of time, it was getting easier for me to cope up the matter regarding Goldie and love. I used to be happy working, going out and living life in an independent manner. But during the night, thoughts and memories of Goldie still haunted me. Somebody had truly said that once you put your head on the pillow, thoughts of various kinds are sure to dominate your mind. But, I decided to be strong and realised that apart from Goldie, there were many other persons who loved me or cared for me and I should live my life for them. There were even many new things to discover, learn and do. I craved for learning more and more and I used to repent sometimes that I had wasted some precious time of my life in Mauritius. Had I been to the United Kingdom earlier, life would have been much different and I would have got a chance to do a lot of new things.

In the month of August, I was invited to the marriage party of a friend of my cousin. So, I accompanied my cousin's family to the marriage registry office at 12 noon where the marriage was being held. It was about 5-6miles from our house. A reception party was thrown at 6p.m. and I was invited as well. I went there as I was feeling very excited to witness a marriage party completely different from our culture, even though the girl was Mauritian. While I was enjoying the party, my eyes fell on my cousin's husband and I saw him talking to an unknown guy sitting next to him. Suddenly, that man turned towards me and said that he was single. I was quite surprised at this approach of his. He went on telling that he was 38 years old and he was working as an engineer under the British railways. He knew that his age was quite more to get married but after seeing all his siblings settle down with their own families, he was too feeling the urge to get married and set up a family. Obviously, I replied in negative and said that I was sorry as I would not be able to accept the proposal because I was 40 years old and in my opinion, it was too much to get married again.

He then took the next step and invited me to dance with him. I felt that my size was almost 18 and I was too fat to dance with him. At this, he started laughing and told me that I was beautiful in my own way. He then came and sat beside me in the empty chair beside me and started conversing. He told me that his name was Brainie. I must give his proposal a second thought and then decide what to do. He said that it was not justified to refuse straightway as by doing that, I might be keeping myself as well as him devoid of justice and charms of life.

He went of giving as much information about himself as he can. He said that he possessed a house of his own, a brand new Audi car and he used to work overtime most of the days so he was able to earn quite a handsome salary. So, it was not required for me to do any work and he guaranteed that I would be very happy at his hands. He said that it must be very tough for me to come up with all the expenses as I had to work hard for collecting the fees of my computer course and I had other needs as well. He also didn't forget to mention that I possessed many good qualities for which he had been yearning. So, it would be better for me to accept his proposal as by doing that, I could live in England as a British citizen and lead a happy and blissful married life.

He wanted to exchange phone numbers but as I refused, he gave his phone number to my cousin and requested her to try to convince me after going back home. So, the next day, she, another cousin and two of my friends came to my house for having a talk on that matter. I told them that I still had feelings for Goldie and we were not divorced till then. The next day was a Monday and in the afternoon, my friend came over to inform me that I had a phone call in her room and I should go to receive it. We used to live in a shared house and I went to receive the call. I could recognise the voice of Brainie on the other side very well and he told me that he had called up to know my decision. I said that it was a "no" from my side and I knew that it was not good news for him.

That afternoon, my auntie too paid a visit to me and while we were talking, I mentioned the name of Brainie before her. I also gave information regarding his address and job. On hearing all these, my auntie was quite surprised and broke the news that I must not go for that man as she used to be a friend of Brainie's mom till her death and that Brainie was divorced and had a daughter. I was totally shocked after acknowledging these and I could not make out how people could dream of planning a future by taking the support of lies from the very first. I asked my auntie not to worry as I would handle him next time he met me.

It was on Wednesday that week when he called up for the second time. He again asked about my decision and I told him directly that I was aware of the lies that he told me. He said that he was very sorry for doing that and he had been feeling guilty since then. He said that he wanted to meet me so that he could ask for an apology and he would be waiting for me at the town bus stop one day after his work was over.

In the coming Monday, when I got off the bus, I saw him waiting for me in his car. The traffic warden was arguing with him to move from that place. He told that he would be parking his car on the roadside before coming to talk to me. He approached me and in the meantime, I gave a call to my friend that I was in the nearby cinema theatre and she need not be worried as I would be late in reaching home. Brainie asked me to get inside his car as it was a breezy day and sensing my hesitation, he said that there was nothing to get afraid as there were lots of people around us. So, I got in and he told me that after calling me and hearing my refusal, he also called up my sister and she only gave him the advice to have a talk with and settle things.

He said that as I was too married, I must had the experience about that and that experience of mine must had let me know that marriages don't work properly all the time. His case was no different and that was why he broke up with his first wife. He was afraid that I might refuse him straight way so he did lie to me, but afterwards he would have revealed everything. He was pleading with me, rather begging me to give him a chance to prove him. He told me that he would be a great husband and I would not regret but at first, I should give him a chance. When I turned my face towards him, I could see tears in his eyes.

I melted a little and told him that the reason behind my refusal is that I had not been able to forget my husband till then and it would not be possible for me to replace his place in my heart. Even if I agreed to marry, I could not guarantee that a day was sure to come on which I would start loving Brainie. So, he could not blame me then if it didn't work out. And he must not pressurize me to love him. It would be all my decision. I revealed that I had a soft heart and I could not see anyone in tears and if it was the wish of God to rebuild my life by being pitiful rather than loving someone, and then let it be. By that time, I also had started crying.

After I returned home, I could see my friend standing in the doorway waiting for me. I explained the entire matter to her and she told me that it would be easy for us to rebuild our lives. I said that things are not always the same as we want as life has its own way to test someone. I was making the sacrifices for his sake and she would have faith on me that I would not let anyone go down.

The next he called me, I replied in affirmative which made him very happy and he said that he would be helping me to obtain my divorce as early as possible. So, as per that we went on looking for a solicitor in the next morning and he told me that as I was staying away from my husband for so long, it would be easier to obtain the divorce. So, we filled in all the forms quickly and we had to pay half of the fees to the solicitor then only. He said he would be paying for that which made me feel that he was a nice and generous guy. After coming back from the solicitor's office, I went to my nephew's place to request so that he called up my mom and gave her the news.

I was aware that a problem may arise as Brainie's grandfather was Scottish while his father was a Christian from my country, even though his mom was a Hindu like me. At first, my mom refused but she was convinced by my nephew as he told her that religions were not followed strictly in the United Kingdom. Finally, she gave in. As soon as she agreed to my marriage, Brainie asked me to move in with him. But I turned down the request as it was beyond my principles to live with someone under one roof and sleep with him before marrying him. At this he told me that as we had applied for an emergency divorce we would be getting that in less than a month and therefore, we would be celebrating our marriage on 11th of September, 1993. I agreed to that and he told me that we would be inviting all friends and relatives at the reception party only. Before that he was going to pay for the ticket so that my mom could come over here to witness the marriage. After the reception was over, we started living like a married couple.

CHAPTER-7:
Plights Continued To Envelope My Life

Both he and I were aware of the fact that I would not be quitting my job even after marriage. Although he had promised me before marriage that it was not required for me to do any work, he asked me continuing working till the end of that year. Every Friday, I used to receive my wage which was 160 pounds that time and I had to hand over the entire amount to my husband. It was so because he felt that I didn't realise the value of money and as he was my husband, I need not take interest in any sort of expenses. He used to give me 10 pounds from that and keep the rest. Those 10 pounds was meant for my bus fare which were 7.50 pounds at that time. The rest 2.50 pounds were my pocket money. I stopped going to school and my visa was about to expire. I had to go back to Mauritius before that. It was like that I had to stay there for a month, then come back, stay in England for six months and then go back again. On the very day, I came to live with him as his wife; he told me that I had no right to open or check his letters or ask him any questions regarding money.

It was the month of March in 1994, when I received my divorce papers. When he returned home from his workplace, I showed him those. He suddenly fell at my feet and said that he wanted to confess something. What he said was enough to take my breath away. He told me that he had married a girl in 1993 just on papers and she went back to her country and was not willing to divorce him then. I was completely shaken and did not know what to do. He said that I could have her phone number, rang and talk to her as she was also a Mauritian.

I called her up and had a talk with her. I came to know from her that their marriage was not at all fake. It was a real marriage and he beat her up just after three months of marriage. But I felt she was a kind lady as after talking to me she said that she could realise my condition and needed some time to think over the matter. I again called her after few weeks and asked her if she would be kind enough to have a word with my husband. She agreed to that and told my husband that she was not going to do anything; because he was british. So, we left the house, gave it on rent and went to leave in another house.

As days went on, Brainie started changing drastically. He started beating me up every now and then, he would complain about every simple thing, and he accused me of not being able to do any work. He even threatened me if I was not more careful, he would send me back to Mauritius and only then I would get a lesson as my relatives and friends would be blaming me for the breaking of marriage. He used to scare me, bully me and even told me that no one was going to listen to me even if I reported against him. As I was only a visitor, no one was going to believe me.

One day, I was talking with his sister-in-law and while talking, she told me that I was the fourth wife of Brainie. He married for the first time in 1979 and he got divorced in the year of 1986. He remarried in 1993 only and again got divorced. After that he married me. The only reason behind these break ups were just domestic violence. He used to beat them up often. She also told me that it was very stupid of me to marry him as one day he would kick me out after taking away all my money and assets as he had done in the other three cases after the parents of his spouses were dead. She consoled me by saying that I must not think that I was similar to the others and face Brainie. I must stand up against his cruelty and shrewdness. I was so scared after listening to all these that I told her that I was going to tolerate all these.

In the year of 1998, when I was in Mauritius he called me up and informed that he would be coming there shortly after. He reached after 15 days and we got civilly married in Mauritius. After that, I was able to obtain a spouse visa which would last for two years. We went back to England on 4th of June. I had by then started planning for our future. I decided to find a proper job and start working again. The next day, as the phone rang, I went to answer it. On the other side, a female voice was talking to me and asked me for Brainie and who I was. I told her that I was his wife. On hearing that, she replied that she was his girlfriend. They had met through an advertisement and had been dating each other. She even spent a few weekends at our house, maybe when I was not there as Brainie had told her that he was not married.

The girl went on telling that they went back to her house and spent a few days there. On the eve of his departure, he asked her to cook a meal for him. As it was already late, she refused to do that. So, there was a hot talk and he left her place in anger. After that he had neither called her nor talked to her. That was why, she came to meet him at our place only to find the door locked and his car parked outside. She enquired the neighbours about him and they told her that he had gone on a holiday. To be sure, she called up at his workplace and they too confirmed that saying that he would be joining work again on 6th of June. After hearing the whole story, I said that we had been since long. When Brainic was back from his work in the evening, he asked in a smiling face if any one called up that day. I answered sarcastically that it was his mistress who called to which he replied that she was no more than a friend. To be very frank, I didn't feel jealous at all. In fact, I felt nothing. I had become so used to be betrayed each time that it was not enough to move me. I felt that if he was happy with that and let me be happy, then it would be better for me to respect the idea.

After that day, our lives changed. We, rather I started to save for the future. I started working in a warehouse and I was no more a fool to hand over that wage. I used to save them. Ever since I had come to England, my only ambition was to work either in the British railways or for the royal mail. Each time, I asked him whether there was any vacancy, he would reply back in negative. By the end of that year, we went for a holiday and we came back in January. One day he ordered to fetch something from his bag and while searching, I obtained a monthly list of vacancies from his bag. I gave the list to him in a cool manner and asked him whether he could get me an application for the post of a cleaner. He told me that he could do that if I gave him 5 pounds.

So, I handed over the amount to him and I got an application form that day. I applied for the job and posted it. After that, came the phase of waiting. I had to wait for a long time patiently and during that time, my life was absolutely boring. I had nothing to do except, cooking, washing, ironing, shopping and working as per his orders. He would come back from his office every day and would sit lazily without doing anything and waiting for me to make his coffee. I was often beaten up by him if I dared not to accomplish his orders.

His brothers and sisters-in-law warned me that I must not disobey as he was such a person who could even kill me if he got angry. That much violence was filled in him. So, I continued to be tolerant towards his each and every form of mental as well as physical torture and pretended not to be stressed out. It was the end of September, when I received a letter from the British railways. It said that if I was interested in the job till then, I should call them. I rang them the next day and was summoned for an interview. It went well and I was selected for the specified position in the month of December. I received the confirmation letter. Before joining, I was to go through a course at the Cambridge College from 4th of January which would last for a week. I continued to work in the warehouse till December.

I started taking preparations for 4th of January. It was a great day for me. I was very excited and I woke up quite early that day as I had to travel a long way by train. It was almost two hours from where we lived. I enjoyed the journey as well as the course. Even though I was to do the job of cleaning, I was required to be literate, to be able to converse with people fluently and the course I was doing was based on customer care services.

After the course was over, I started working in a station in capital city of London. I used to work very hard but as I enjoyed doing the job, I never felt stressed out. I worked overtime most of the days. As a result, I would be out from my house at 5:30a.m and it got almost 6:30p.m when I reached home. After going back, I had to do the entire household chores, cooking, washing and making coffee for us as usual. He asked me to open a joint account with him so that we could deposit and save together. He said that by doing that, we would also be able to spend whenever we liked. As I had no interest in anything in my life, I agreed to whatever he said.

When we received our wages at the end of the month, it went to the joint account. He said that as I was working to save for our future, I should not waste money on anything. If I had to buy something, I should ask him and then only buy it. As I was a woman who was not after cosmetics or fancy make up kits, it was not difficult for me to obey him.

From the next month, he stopped working during the extra hours and when he received his salary, it was just his flat pay for the time from 8:30a.m to 3:30p.m. When I compared his payslip with mine, I was surprised to see that I earned almost two times more than him. I was not happy with that and asked him to work harder else I would stop working over hours. He told me that there were not ever meant to work over time in their office and I believed him. I was not aware that by the end of August I had already saved 9000 pounds. I was paying all the bills which consisted of phone bills, gas, electricity bills and used to all the shopping for the household at my own expense. He used to pay the mortgage of only 600 pounds for both our houses. On the other hand, he was also receiving the rent of 800 pounds. So, he was quite well off than me. I pursued him to pay for the car insurance and petrol so that it was easy for me to go to work. But he didn't ever let me do that as he paid those bills.

I was so stupid and dumb that I used to keep my mouth shut just because I was scared of him. I could not gather courage to go against his autocracy. But as I was working in London, I had developed quite a good friend by that time, and I could make out that their married life was not at all similar to me. They used to tell me that it was my stupidity to follow each and everything he said. Everybody was free in the country and in England; things were much different from the ones in Mauritius. They told me that I must make Brainie feel that I was earning more than him, and therefore, he would help with the household chores. Whenever they use to see bruise marks on my cheeks, they asked about them and each time I lied. At last, with the help of my manager, I was able to find out that Brainie was not an engineer, but only a cleaner in his depot and his salary was equivalent to me. When I asked him about that, he flatly said that he lied to me so that it became easy for him to convince me to marry him.

It was one afternoon when I came back home and he informed me that I had a savings of 9000 pounds and asked me if we could buy a house together. I refused straight way. He was not happy at all. The next day, during my lunch break, I went to the bank to enquire about my account and saw that only his salary of the first month was deposited there. The rest had been transferred by him to his personal account. When I returned home, I asked him about the fact and blamed him for not asking me before doing that, to which he said that he was not a fool like me who didn't know the actual value of money. Later on, that day, he also convinced me to buy that house. He told me that we could put that on rent and therefore, there would be no worry of paying the mortgage. So, we bought a house having a mortgage of 268 pounds, whereas we received 800 pounds as rent.

Honestly speaking, I was not at all aware of where all my savings were or what he was doing with that money. At the end of December we went for my brother's wedding ceremony, and he asked me for money as he didn't have. I was so angry that I refused to give him a single penny. We had a big argument over that and I opened my mouth before him for the first time. I said I would live with him just like a slave or a money producing machine. He had to give me the status of a wife in his life and he was extremely displeased with that.

When we came back home that day, I told him that I wanted to sleep in the guest room and there will be nothing between us from that day. Gradually I learnt from various sources that he has many girlfriends although he was married to me. I started hating myself for my foolishness. How could I bear that for so long! My conscience told me that it was time for thinking and spending on me and getting justice. I could no longer bear this slavery. It was time to hit back. Life was as usual. As soon as I would come back from office, he would place his order for coffee. Then I had to make food and call him for dinner. He was living like a king, always lazing around or watching T.V. as if the whole day was meant for leisure. He was in in the habit of dominating his wife as was the culture in our country long time ago. At that time, women were not allowed to work outside. So, the man of the house was to do a job and feed his family and, that was why, doing any household work was restricted to them. But society changed their views afterwards. Women were being given the same privilege as men. Although Brainie was born and brought up in England and neither was he working to feed me, his attitude towards women was bad as long before.

Nothing in our life changed. One day when I was working, my eyes fell on a local paper and I started reading that. There was an advertisement seeking women for fun. While I was going through that, I remembered that I had seen a same piece of paper at my home. That day, I came back early and started searching for that bit of paper which I finally obtained from Brainie's room. I took the phone number and called up only to hear Brainie's voice pleading with someone to ring him. I didn't know what I was doing in his life. I was shocked and I made up my mind to stop all these bullshit. I should be filing a divorce. I had tapped the call and when he came back, I put the phone on loudspeaker and let him hear his voice, and asked for explanation. He denied straightway that it was his voice. I said that he had crossed all levels of my patience and I decided that I should go for a divorce.

When I went to work next day, I told my friend all about that and she told me that it was time for me to file in a divorce as it had been almost seven years of life of slave. So, I took an appointment with a solicitor and she told me that it would be taking about 15 days. But on the eve of the day on which we were having the appointment, at about 9p.m, I had to answer a knock. It was an usher from the court who had brought me a divorce paper on Brainie's him. I got inside and told him that I was happy with that. I took that paper and went to meet my solicitor next day. She told me that if both sides agree, it could be a mutual divorce which would be very easy to get. And it was quite true.

I was very happy but was quite worried about the financial part. I went for a solicitor who could fight for me and he said that he would charge 3000 pounds. I gave 1000 pounds to him and said that I would be paying the rest of the amount in instalments. After two weeks I received a paper from him which said that Brainie was offering the second house to me and that was all he was giving me. I went to the court two times just along with my barrister without any documents from my solicitor. The court told me the first time that my solicitor would be paying the fees and, next time they told me that it was me who was to pay the fees. I realise that he was going to do nothing for me and I decided to change my solicitor. When I went to meet him, he promised me to deal with the case at first and then we can summon another solicitor. He charged me 3000 pounds. I offered to pay 1500 pounds in cheque and the rest afterwards. He agreed to that and told me that he would me writing to another lawyer for my papers in a few days.

When I returned to my house that day, I was surprised to found the entrance door of my house broken. Later I came to know that it was my ex-husband who did that, and he had taken loads of things from the house. I was so angry that I called up the cops. But they told me that it was not possible for them to do anything as he was the owner of the house. They called for a locksmith and made him repair the lock, and advised me to ask my solicitor to help me. I called up my lawyer and even though he said he would some action, nothing happened. In the meantime, my husband broke the main door twice and still the police was of no help to me. Finally, after two months, I got a call from my lawyer and he informed me that I had to appear at the court in two days. It was very short notice and we were running out of time to prepare anything. I was so tired and frustrated of going to the court that I told him to say to my husband's solicitor that I would be happy with whatever I get from him.

Renooka Gopaul

I received the house in which I was living in along with a mortgage of 68,000 pounds. After that I went to meet my solicitor who charged me 1200 pounds for writing my papers. I asked him whether I could summon another solicitor. He told me that I was very lucky to have his house which was worth 110,000 pounds and we could have gone for another solicitor if we had money. But I had run out of all my resources by that time.

I was so hurt and disappointed with my life that I could not go to or concentrate on any work. I had also started taking anti depression tablets. I could not sleep at night. So, I consulted a doctor who advised me to go for a counselling session. I followed his advice and those sessions helped me a lot in recovering from the mental trauma I was going through. It was around September when I started becoming normal in due course of time and starting going to work. I again earned my own living and was able to stand on my own feet. Gradually I was forgetting my past life and I understood the reality of life. God was with me and I was able to fulfil all my responsibilities. I was happy as I possessed my job and had a house of my own.

CHAPTER-8:
Third Time Lucky?

In the month of June 2002, my mum's sister and niece were coming over to spend their holidays and to attend the wedding in Ireland. They had decided to stay over at my place for about a month. I surely had enough place to accommodate them since I had my two bedroom house that we bought in 1996, but although it was furnished, it needed decoration like carpeting, painting, and of the sort. I needed to look for somebody who would decorate the house before my mum's arrival. That alone wouldn't suffice; at that time I had been having changing shifts at work—some days I would finish early and on others I would go on till late night, so I needed someone whom I could trust and leave the house keys with. I called my nephew and asked him if he knew someone who could help me and was trustworthy at the same time. He assured he would and arrived with his friend the following Sunday as promised.

He had also brought a friend of his friend who was not working anywhere and was looking for a job to earn his means. He agreed to help me paint and decorate the house the following week onwards. It was March then and I told him that I would wish to have the house ready by May. He agreed to it, but quite contradictorily he didn't show up for the next two weeks. I called my nephew up and asked for his number. He didn't have the number but said he would see what could be done. The next day he called me back with this piece of information: The person's name was Dave and he would come to see me as soon as possible; he hadn't been feeling well enough to start work.

A few more days passed before he finally called me up in mid-April and told me that he would come to see me. He arrived as promised and explained that he had lost his cell phone. I told him that I would give her a cell phone to use for the time being. He then assured me that he would take over the work at my house from the next Monday. He had already been late for his job and needed a week in between to complete it. He was a Mauritian like me in this foreign land, and I didn't feel uneasy to trust him; so I agreed.

The following Sunday, Dave called me and said that he would start working the next day onwards. I had to leave for work at 5:30 am and so I needed to find a way to give him the key to my house when he arrived. I suggested that I would leave the key in a flower pot wrapped up in a tissue before leaving for work. The next day it was raining when I left. I was a little apprehensive about leaving my house to a relative stranger; so I called my neighbor at 10 am and asked if he was there in my house. She said no. I told her to pick up the key from where I had left it since it wasn't safe there. I was upset and decided that I wouldn't let Dave do the job since he was so irresponsible. He called me up at night and promised to come the next day. I didn't agree initially and made it clear that I wasn't happy with him. But I yielded to his requests finally and told him to meet me the next day.

He arrived on the following day and explained why he hadn't been able to appear. I could see how desperate he was to get the job. I melted and jokingly suggested and he shouldn't lie and should be serious next time around. He promised to come and start his work. When he left, I felt a soft corner growing in my heart for this stranger—as if I had pity for him and wanted to give him another chance even though he hadn't shown even an iota of responsibility before.

Contrary to all his promises, he didn't show up the next day. I was really upset now and decided not to call him or receive his calls thereafter. Two days later, when I returned from work, my neighbor informed me that Dave had come, worked and left. The next day I returned early from work to meet him and explain that I had already fixed the carpet. We met up the next day and he smiled and asked "Are you still angry with me?" "Why should I be?" was my counter question. He shrugged his shoulders and said "I have loads of problems in my life. One day I shall tell you". I looked at him inquisitively for a while.

Dave, his friend who had accompanied him the other day, I and my friend—the four of us had dinner together that night. We talked a lot, got to know each other better, and spend around 2 hours of quality time. That very day onwards, Dave had been regular at his work. He would often ask me what shift I had at work. If I had late shift, he would assure me that he would wait for me till I returned. I would come home, we would have dinner together and he would tell me about himself.

He said that he had a son in Mauritius who lived with his mum. Dave had come here to earn a new life so that he could secure a bright future for his son and himself. He was a divorcee and had come here on a leave without pay from his job as a prison officer. He had even just finished a course concerning prison duty. He also told me that he had no place of his own to live in; he stayed with some friends in a warehouse storage and sometimes they could afford nothing better than baked beans for lunch and dinner.

I felt like sympathizing with him having learnt about the hurdles in his life. I told him that from the next day onwards he could make his breakfast and lunch at my place itself. At night, I would cook dinner for the both of us. Thus, slowly but surely, I had started to open up to him. I told him about my dreadful past in bits and pieces. He showed compassion and said that I had been unlucky to have gone through many more difficulties than he had. He even assured me that he would be a good friend and would help me as much as he could.

He started doing my shopping while I worked. He had undoubtedly become a part of my life. Many people would think that it's impossible for a man and a woman to be best friends, especially when they are on the same boat. I would have disagreed to that at this juncture of my life. However, I observed that Dave had become very slow with the job. But I said nothing, and assured myself that we had time till the end of 22nd June.

As days passed by, we came closer and closer. It was as if he knew everything concerning my life and my house. I trusted him with every household job, and just gave him the money. I had started to feel lighter—as if a heavy burden had been shared. On the 20th of June, I returned from work and was very upset to find that the job had not been finished yet. The next day, he worked till 1:00 am to finish painting, yet not being able to complete the task. He went back home and arrived at 5:00 am again to take me to the airport so that I could escort my guests to my place. It was a Sunday. We needed two cars for all of us. Upon reaching home, I invited all my cousins, sisters, brother in law and relatives for a dinner that very day.

As Dave was leaving, my mum told me to ask Dave to come and join us. I did, but he refused saying he was too tired. All of us spent a great time in the evening. The next day, as I was leaving for work, Dave told me that if I didn't mind, he would like to show the guests around. I agreed and I called him that night to ask if he could make it the next day. He was positive and I left for work at 5:30 am in the morning, feeling assured. In order to spend time with the guests, I had decided to do my default hours at work only—no overtime for the week. I reached home after 3 pm only to find that none was home. I cooked dinner for all in the meantime. When they returned, everyone seemed happy and was all praises for Dave. They said he was a nice man; he had done this and he had done that for them. I thought to myself that they knew nothing about him, and it was I who was taking care of the expenses.

The wedding which was the focal point of their visit was to be held on the 28th of June, a Friday, in Ireland. My sister and niece went on Wednesday while my mum went on Thursday. On the afternoon of Thursday, after I returned from work, Dave called me up and asked if he could pop in. He arrived, and straightaway asked me to go to the pub with him. They played live Indian music in that pub. I denied with the excuse that I had to go for work early the next day. He asked me whether I was afraid to go out with him alone; if so, I could call my neighbor and ask her if she was interested. She agreed straightaway and soon I heard her knock at my door. I told them that they could go if they wished, but I wasn't interested. Dave insisted saying he knew I would be upset being alone at home after spending a few days with everyone; so he wanted to make me a little chilled out. My neighbor convinced me as well. I had to give in finally, on the condition that we came back early. Dave agreed and said he would come at 8 pm to pick us all up. I went out with Dave, my neighbor, and her nephew.

As I was about to board the car, Dave opened the front door and asked me to get in. I was pretty surprised but said nothing. In the pub, we started with a snack and a drink, and then had dinner. They really had live Indian music playing and he quietly requested a love song for me. He sent a text message to tell me this, lest my neighbor found out. The song was lovely—we had a great time and came back home. Back home, Dave had coffee and I noticed certain abnormalities in his behavior. It seemed as if he wanted to let me know about some hidden feelings of his. I tried to put him off many times, and even changed the topic or simply acted stupid to avoid his overtures.

69

I was adamant not to give him any chance of saying something. Eventually he called it a night and left.

Two days later, my mum, sister and niece were supposed to come back and Dave promised to come and pick us up at the station. I called him up; he was waiting when he arrived. Back home, mum cooked and all of us had dinner. Later on, we were planning about our hereabouts on the coming Sunday, when he chipped in telling us not to worry since he would be there. I was free that day so I accompanied all of them to the city. The following day was my brother's birthday and he was visiting UK for just 3 days coming back from the wedding. I wanted to put up a surprise birthday party for him at my residence and planned accordingly. I invited all our relatives, and about thirty of us were supposed to gather. Dave insisted that he would cook for the party. So I left for work, and when I returned they were nowhere to be seen.

I was quite upset since I felt we would be late for the party. They arrived soon after and everyone started helping us arrange things in time. Dave cooked the main dish—fried rice. The party was happily over soon and all the invitees had returned home. I could hear my mum and sister talking about Dave, saying he was caring and helpful, and that he was a really nice guy. As I went to bed that night, I thought to myself "Is he doing all this for me? Must be so, and if he ever needs help, I shall be there for him".

The next afternoon, the two of us were preparing food when they came home. Dave excused himself saying he had to leave early since he had to drop off his friend who was going to Mauritius. As he left, everybody seemed to be missing him a lot. He was becoming a part of every conversation. At about 10 pm he rang me and said that the owner of the warehouse where he lived was that friend's brother, and he had locked the door. So he had nowhere to go. I consulted my mum and she said that he could come and spend the night on the sofa in the lounge. I rang him back and asked him to come. But he refused saying he was with a friend. However, he promised to come the next morning.

The next morning, as he arrived, I asked him whether he wanted to rent a room. He answered in the affirmative. I suggested that he could rent the vacant room in my neighbor's house. He went to talk with my neighbor, and when he came back, he asked me whether he could borrow £100 from me as the deposit amount. I was surprised; it was very abnormal, I thought, to come to rent a house without any money. However, I wrote him a cheque which the landlord accepted and handed him over the keys. He had no belongings with him since everything all that had been left out at the warehouse. So I thought I should help him in whatever way I could. I told him that he could have breakfast, lunch and dinner with us as my guest from the next day. I would allow that since he neither had a job nor money. But he would have to find a job as soon as possible.

I was that day onwards that Dave became literally a part of my family. I considered him to be nothing more than just a friend. I had an unmarried friend and I had often told Dave to consider marrying her and settle down. He refused saying he had no intention of marrying anyone. Every day he used to go out with my guests while I worked during the weekdays. I abstained from doing overtime and reserved my weekends for spending time with them. On Sunday, the 13th of July, my sister and niece were supposed to leave UK and return to Mauritius. We went to the airport to see them off while I noticed that Dave had been talking to my sister quietly about something. I had no idea what he was talking about.

The next day after my sister left, I was suffering from a back pain and so I went to see my doctor. He suggested that I should take a few days' rest so that I recovered well. I took leave and was home every day with my mum. Dave hadn't been able to find any work by then, and I had to give him money every week for his room. One day, we were supposed to go to my sister's place to drop my mum. He was still sleeping in his room. So I went to his room and knocked at his door. He answered my knock and told me to come inside.

This was the first time that I had entered his room. He was still lying on the bed. As I went closet, to my utter surprise, he pulled me on to the bed! I was extremely upset and embarrassed, and cried out to him "What are you doing?" He seemed to be nonchalant and said with conviction "I love you. I love you too much! I want to marry you!" I was awe-struck at this sudden development. "No!" I replied, pulling myself together. "Do you know how old I am?" I asked. "Age is a number for me", he said. "I don't care", he continued "I love you and I want to be with you my whole life." I was pretty taken aback and said to myself "No more of this thing". I pulled myself away from him, turned towards him and said "I have no intention to marry or even have a relationship." Then I turned away and ran.

He came to my house a while later after the incident. I told him to drop my mum where she wanted to go; I wouldn't come since I had lots of other things to do. He left and did as I said without uttering a word. Then he called me up and asked me to go out with him. I refused straightaway, but he kept insisting saying he had to talk to me. So I finally relented and agreed. I wore an evening dress that day. When he saw me in that dress, he said "Look at you in the mirror. Is there any way you look 49 years old?" The wall of my dining room was made of a huge mirror. He brought me in front of that and said "Look if there is any difference between us. Can you tell if I am younger than you?" I didn't reply. But I said to myself "He's right, I look young for my age."

We went out to the pub. As it was already very late, we just had time for a drink and then had to return. At home, he started the conversation. He said "Look Pearl, I know you have been very unlucky in your life. You told me in the morning that you don't need anybody in your life. But please try to think in this fashion: if you got two bad husbands, it doesn't mean that the third one won't be good. He might finally bring luck and happiness to you." I replied saying "Sorry I can do nothing about it. To be honest, even if you love me till eternity, I can never love you back. I shall never be able to love you in the way you love me. I surely want to help you out, but not in this way." He said "I will give you time to think." From that day onwards, I started to grow a little bit of love for him in my heart. But I was determined not to let my heart beat my brain.

One day, my neighbor came to see me at my home. She told my mum to inform me that my other friend and she would wait for me that night. They wanted to see me. After we had our dinner, Dave left and I said to my mum "I am going next door to see my friend." When I met the two of them, I realized that Dave had told them about his feelings for me and that I had refused him. He had told them to try and explain to me what a good turn my life would take if I married him; my luck would finally change after so many years of sorrow. They tried long and hard to convince me. They said "In this country, nobody cares about age, or other people's lives. For everybody, if they are happy, that's it." Finally I stirred a little from my stance and told them "Tell him to ask my mum. I shall do as my mum says. No argument, no stubbornness. I shall gladly accept whatever my mum decides."

The next morning, Dave came, had his breakfast as usual, and said to us he is going to see a job at his other friend's place and left. When he returned, we had lunch in the garden. Afterwards, my mum said she was going to watch TV and left. I and he were alone now. He asked me to tell him honestly what had happened the previous night. "I do feel something for you," I replied "but everything will depend on my mum's decision."

Eventually, just before going to work, he popped the question to my mum. She asked him "Do you know her age? What are you going to do with your son?" He seemed poised and said "Age is nothing but a figure. I love her too much, and as Pearl doesn't have a kid, we shall be a complete family with my son. I can promise you that she will be the happiest wife in the world. I shall care for her and love her so much that she forgets the past. I shall ensure that she achieves whatever she has expected out of her life". My mum seemed satisfied with the conviction in his voice. She said "It's okay if it is so. Since Pearl is happy with this, you can have my blessings." He left with his lips bent in a subtle smile.

CHAPTER-9:
Happily Married For A While

After all my relatives had left after the reception, we started living our lives to the fullest. We went to see a solicitor so that he could help us in settling there. When we were filling in the required forms, I came to know that his visa had already expired. The solicitor told us that he could help us in obtaining his visa, but he would be charging 350 pounds for that. I paid that amount then and there as I wanted Dave to obtain his visa as soon as possible. The solicitor told us that he will be sending his documents to the home office shortly afterwards. As he was not able to work, I had to work even harder and do more overtime for making all the ends meet. Dave used to stay at the house all the day, waiting eagerly for the time when he would be able to apply for his N.I. number, so that he could start working at the earliest.

It was the first week of October. One day he came to pick up at the London railway station after my work time was over. On the way, he told me that he had got something important to discuss with me. He told that my relatives had started to talk negatively about our marriage. They were saying that they could sense the darker sides of our marriage, and that he had married me only for two reasons, to make money and to get the citizenship of England so that he could settle here. Both he and I were very upset on hearing such things from my relatives and he told me that he loved me too much and didn't want anything from me. He had married me so that he could make me happy and we had a healthy married life. I believed him as I too had feelings for him. He asked me whether we could leave London and go to live somewhere else. I agreed to his proposal.

He said that he would be looking for a shop as it was his ambition to be self-employed, and if he succeeded in owning a shop, his dreams would be fulfilled and there would be no boss over his head. I supported his idea and went for work the next day. After I came back, he told me that he had two options in his hands; one was a paper shop in Liverpool and the other one was at Blackpool. There was a huge difference in price. As compared to Liverpool, Blackpool was a bit backward and that was why, the cost of the shop at Liverpool was 2000 pounds more. I was not that much interested in Blackpool. He said that he had taken appointment with the owner at Blackpool and we two would be going for an inspection on the coming Saturday. He also said that he had booked two tickets for us in the national express coach.

Though I was not sure about settling in Blackpool, I trusted him. He was my world then. I wanted to live for him so, we went over there. We talked with the owner and I liked the area so I approved the idea of buying the shop and settling there. We promised the owner that we would let him know our decision. On Monday, I called up my solicitor and let him know my decision to re-mortgage my house so that I could buy the shop. All the things went according to my plans and I bought the shop in cash. After that, I went to inform my neighbour that we were shifting to Blackpool. She warned me that I should give it a second thought. As all my relatives were staying in London, it would be ideal for me to dwell in London only. She told me that I had started trusting Dave too early and we would be only the two at Blackpool.

But it was already too late and things could not be changed. We were going to shift on 16th of November, 2002. I was only two and half months married to Dave at that time. The day we shifted was a great day for me. We moved all our things to the small two bedrooms flat at Blackpool. The flat was situated at the top of the shop. The shop was just a corner shop which used to sell only essential things of daily need like paper, cigarettes and milk. It seemed very small to me. Dave had great plans for renovating our shop. We used to plan to transform our shop into a supermarket, and he would often say that we had to do this and that, never bothering how we were going to afford the expenses. As every year, I used to do, that year too, I planned for my holidays at the end of the year. As a result, we could not start anything about renovation before January, 2003. I was going to Mauritius on 15th of December so; I called up my solicitor to get back my passport. He told me that I would receive the passport before my date of journey. But I had to return it back as there was a big problem at the home office.

Anyways, I received my passport on 12th of December and I left on 15th, providing him with a lady to help him in the shop. He used to call me every day and he cried bitterly as he used to miss me. He pleaded with me to come back at the earliest but I could not return as my ticket was a promotional one and it would cost extra charges if I returned early.

When I left England on 15th of December, he asked me to go and meet his parents as well as son over here in Mauritius. 23rd December was his son's birthday and I bought two gifts for him, one for his birthday and another one for Christmas. I also bought Christmas presents for his parents. I went to meet them on 22nd of December. I didn't know anything except the address. His dad came to open the door. He greeted me and both he and my mother-in-law were kind to me. They accepted my gifts and informed me that Dave's son was residing with his mom. I spent five minutes with them as the driver was waiting for me.

On 5th of January, I got a call from my in-laws and they asked me if I could have lunch with them. I was very happy as well as excited and accepted the invitation. I went there and I had a nice time with them eating together and chatting to our hearts' content. They told me that used to miss their eldest son, Dave. He had three other siblings, two sisters and one brother. His sisters were married and his brother used to work outside so they felt lonely in their old age. I felt sorry for them. Before I bade goodbye to them, I asked them if they would like to visit England and meet their son. They were overjoyed to hear that and told me that would like to do so.

As his parents were doing job, they had to give notice in advance for taking leave. So, we planned that they could come to England in June and we all would have a good time together. I also said that I would be paying for their tickets. They were very happy and moved by this.

After returning to England, I told Dave that his parents were planning to visit England sometime in June and meet him. He told me that he had already called up his parents and they told that I had paid a visit to them and I was going to pay for their tickets. Afterwards he said that he had got something to tell me. He told that his parents had praised me much. They had said that they liked me very much and didn't about my age at all. They were sure that I would prove to be a very good wife and their son would be happy. I was filled with joy to the brim and felt quite proud, and said to him lovingly that they loved him so much and he used to be scared for no reason, fearing something wrong would happen.

By the end of January, we started to renovate the shop. We worked day and night to make it look like a super market and we were successful in our mission. I had to a course on off license. For being successful in the exam, I had to do a course on accountancy and income tax, so that we would not require keeping other people for maintaining those documents and doing those jobs. This would reduce our expenses to some extent. Dave could not do anything, as he was still waiting for his visa.

By the end of May, I was able to buy a three bedrooms, semi-detached house. I mainly bought that house for accommodating my in-laws when they would come over here. We could have a quiet place then instead of the small flat on the top of the shop. We were busy cleaning and decorating our new house. I started feeling weak. When I paid a visit to the doctor, he told me that it was due to over work, and as my age was above forty, I had started to feel weak because of stress, depression, diabetes and arthritis. It was really very cold in Blackpool. He advised me not to work so hard. So, I stopped doing that but still I used to help Dave with his shop as far as I could.

In June 2003, we had to keep the shop closed for one whole day as his parents was arriving. We had to go to receive them at Heathrow Airport. On the day, they arrived; they went to stay at flat on the top of the shop, as we had to open the shop in the wee hours of the morning. On Sundays, we used to close the shop at 12:30 p.m. on Sunday, they went to our new house. They kept themselves busy all day long, as they were helping in cleaning and decorating the house. I remained in the shop with Dave all throughout the day. My work was only to do the cooking. During lunch time, Dave would go to pick up his parents for eating together. His mom would say every day that she must wake up early so that she could help Dave in arranging the newspapers and magazines, and I get some rest.

I used to wake up at 6a.m in the morning and I used to have my breakfast in the shop only. Then I did my deskwork. Whenever he used to go to the warehouse, both his parents would accompany him. I could feel that his mom had been maintaining distance with me for quite some time. When I said Dave about that, he said me jokingly that I was mad. It was true that his mom had a problem with me as my age was more but he had stopped his mom from saying anything further as he loved me very much and I was his world. We were made for each other and our love for each other was eternal.

Next day, nothing worthy of mentioning occurred. As I was a person with a soft heart having good manners and well cultured, I didn't prefer to take revenge on the persons who hurt me. Rather I liked to be patient with them and help them realise their mistakes.

One day, when I was in the shop, his brother called up from Mauritius and asked for his dad. As the phone used to be on my table, I received the call and handed over it to my father-in-law. I could see him went into the kitchen and talked to Dave in a whispering tone. Sensing my surprise, Dave told them that they could speak freely in front of me. What I heard was that a bailiff from Mauritius had called him. He wanted to go to their house for collecting all the furniture next day at 2:30 p.m. as Dave had not paid the mortgage of his house since 2001. I called up the bailiff company and said that Dave was in England and they replied that as the owner had to present during the course they could not do it then so they cancelled it.

That day, Dave's parents told me that he owed a huge sum of money to someone and that was why he had left his country; otherwise they would have put him into jail. His ex-wife was required to go to police station every week to sign because of him. I asked them to give me sometime so that I could think over the matter and work out something. That night, I was having a discussion with him regarding that matter. He told me that whatever his parents had said was true. I said that being a woman, I could very well realise what his ex-wife would be going through in such a situation and I could not accept that mentally. I promised him to re-mortgage a house so that I would be able to collect the money and give it to him.

By the end of July, both my in-laws decided to go back. Before leaving, they said that they were very grateful to me as whatever I was doing for them, only an angel could accomplish all those. After went back, we used to stay in the shop flat only. As our shop was running well and we were doing quite well with the customers, we did that. We used to go to the separate house only on Sundays to clean it and have dinner over there.

In December, 2003, I was going to celebrate my 50th birth anniversary. We had plans for hosting a big party for that occasion. We had invited about fifty guests at our place. But afterwards, some relatives in London said that they were not going to turn up for the party so we had to cancel it. My sister was supposed to come with her two daughters for celebrating the occasion. But as the part was cancelled, she called me up and asked me to go to London so that we can spend the day there and also celebrate. But Dave was not pleased with the new idea.

On 3rd December, he told me that he was going to take me out for dinner after his work in the shop got over. He made to wear the dress he had chosen for me and even forced me to do make up. After I was ready, he took hold of me and made me stand in front of the mirror and asked me if I looked much older. He claimed that I could look no more than 35 years of age. I was delighted and trusted him. In fact, inside, I never felt older than what he had said whenever I was in his arms!

He took me to Hilton Hotel. To my surprise, he had already booked a table for us. When we went to the receptionist, the manager of the hotel guided us to our table and there were two waiters standing there to serve us. The table was decorated nicely with flowers and beautiful table cloth. I could not hold my emotions back and started crying. I was above the ninth cloud seeing the preparations that he did. He held me and said that I must be missing my siblings, relatives and mom on that special day, but he would do something which would make me cherish the day for my entire life. It would be a special day comprising just me and him! We had dinner and then he ordered a bottle of champagne, worth 250 pounds. As I didn't use to drink much, we left the rest of it for the waiters. As I was sitting in such a position such that my back faced the wall, all in a while I could hear the song "Happy Birthday" being sung in chorus. There were lights all around and a cake too. I cut the cake and it was so big that we could have it totally, so we left that too with the waiters. I was very, very happy. I had longed for such a birthday where I would be made to feel like a princess and I was even happier to think that I meant so much to him.

The waiters told us that they were all Mauritians over there. They were hotel management students and they had been working there as trainees. I asked them to come over at our place on Sundays so that we could have lunch together and have a good time chatting and sharing tit-bits. Next Sunday, eight of them, five boys and three girls turned and we had lunch together. I was very happy in their company and I told them, that from that day onwards, I was like their mom.

As I used to do every year, in the beginning of January, I started making preparation for going to Mauritius for celebrating my mom's birth anniversary. That year, I had made arrangements for a long prayer of nine days. I called up the solicitor for obtaining his passport and he said that he would try his to do something. Afterwards, he wrote to me in order to inform that he could not do anything for us as there was still a great backlog. So, I had to leave him and leave for Mauritius. I did that so that I could clear his debts over there and free his ex-wife from the harassment of going to police station and signing every week.

At Mauritius, after the prayer was over, I called up his solicitor over there, and took an appointment with his parents as well as his lender. I went to meet them and handed over half of the payment to the solicitor. I promised him to pay the rest of the when he would take the case from the police. Before giving the cheque, I was advised by his parents not to reveal that I was his wife. Rather, I should introduce myself as a friend. The solicitor told me that he would be starting the very next day. As all the things could not be finalized before I left Mauritius, I deposited the money in his account and let his parents know that.

I returned to England two days after the Valentine's Day that is, on 16th of February. When I reached my house, I could see my card, gift and bouquet waiting for me on the bed! When I opened the card, I saw that it was blank and nothing written on it. I was in a jovial mood and told Dave jokingly that I was sure that he had no love for me that was why; he had left the card blank. He came to me and said lovingly that he was sorry for that; as he was very busy with the shop and his responsibilities, he could not write anything, but he loved me. He said in an emphasizing manner that his love for me grows every day and he loved me more than a day back. I was so happy that we both broke into laughter.

One day we were indulged in a discussion regarding our shop, when he dropped in the suggestion of buying a restaurant as our shop was running well. I suggested that we should see go to his solicitor at first. His visa was required at the earliest and we didn't have that. It had already been two years. To my surprise, he told me that he was going to change his solicitor. Though he had charging much less, he was very slow in his duty. So, we went to London one day in search of a good solicitor. My sister and brother-in-law were requested to help us at our shop as we would not be present. We did find a good solicitor and he said that his charge was 350 pounds, and Dave was supposed to get his visa within a short time. He assured us that we would be receiving the confirmation from him in less than three months. I agreed with him and signed a check in his name. We came and spent another three months waiting patiently. Nothing happened during this time.

A t the end of August, I called him up for enquiring about the visa and he asked Dave to go to him. So, we went on the following Sunday. After reaching there, I told Dave that I was going to lie down as I was feeling uneasy. So, as I rested, he went to talk to the solicitor. I was not feeling well that day. He came back and informed me that he had asked us to wait as it would be taking a bit time. So, we went back to Blackpool. We made up our minds to buy the restaurant. In fact, it was not possible for me to turn down any of his request. Whatever he asked for, I used to oblige. He was my world and I could not think of anything but him. So, I started going through the advertisements in newspapers. I used to go to the Blackpool casino and he would often accompany me there or come to escort me after two hours. He used to say that he was too tired and bored with the shop as it was always busy and he didn't have time to take his breath.

CHAPTER-10:
Dark Clouds

By the end of October that year, he found out a 60 seated luxury restaurant in Bristol and told me about it. He called up the owner and asked for an appointment to visit the property one day. As they were living in Torquay, we planned to meet at Bristol. We went there and did like the restaurant, but the price was a bit too high. Dave was insisting that we buy it and he told me that it was going to make profit. I agreed to pay 15000 pounds to the Chinese couple so that we could start the paper work and other formalities. I decided to re-mortgage a house at London and I went to see my solicitor for that. I had to give him 1000 pounds as he told me that he would be helping me in re-mortgaging. But as our fate could have it, it could not be accomplished. So, I applied for mortgaging a house in Blackpool. By the end of October, we had the keys of the restaurant and we opened it on 17th of November, 2004. But our plan did not succeed. Our restaurant was situated in a residential area, and there were more than ten take-ways in the same street. So, we lost every single we had spent.

After coming back to Blackpool, we started concentrating on the shop even more as it was our only asset. We had to rely on that for paying all the bills and mortgages. We used to work over hours, and still we were late in paying our bills. In January, 2005, I told him that he would start for searching a work desperately as our resources were limited. After much difficulty, he was successful in getting one at home care in February. He had to do quite a few night shifts. One day in March, he told me that he did not want to go to work as it was

Renooka Gopaul

Easter Friday. But I forced him to go as were in utter need of money. Next day, on 26th of March, early morning, at 6:30a.m, I was working at my shop, when two police officers came and informed me that my brother-in-law was arrested in a rape case. I was totally taken aback as my brother-in-law was with me only helping me with my work. I told the police officer about that. After that, at about 6:45a.m, I received a call from Dave. He informed me that he would not be able to come back home that day, as he was going to London with some work. I told him about the entire morning episode and he told me that there had been a problem at his home and cut the line. I sent him infinite number of messages and tried to call him many times but in vain.

He didn't answer a single one of them and I left a few messages. Again at 2:30p.m, the police officers came to meet me and they asked for my permission to search my other house where my brother-in-law was living along with his family. By that time, I had come to know that rape case took place at the care-home where Dave had been working. At 5p.m., when he was leaving, the policeman came and informed me that the crime had been actually committed by Dave and the blame came on my brother-in-law's name as Dave was working on his name. I got the shock of my life. If he had committed the rape, he had brutally raped my faith too. They showed the warrant against him, and asked me to inform them as soon as I received any call from Dave. The voice mailbox was full with messages.

The police again came to see me next morning. It was a Sunday. On that day, they took a statement from me. I promised them to help in the case in every possible way. Finally, on 28th of March, on Monday, Dave was arrested by the police at Tottenham in North London. The jeep which he had been driving was mine. The police called me up to inform that they would be reaching Blackpool by afternoon, and I should arrange someone to escort the jeep from the police station.

I had a sister who was dwelling in North London. She promised to help me in this matter. When Dave arrived in Blackpool, I finally got a chance to speak to him. I called him up and he started crying. He told me in his sobs that he had done nothing wrong. Next morning, he was the hot topic in the radio. He was sent to jail at Preston by the court. The radio announced his name, address and even his nationality. It was a huge setback to our business, as our customers came over and over again to enquire about the truth. I had to tell them what had happened. The policeman asked for his passport and I had to tell them that it was still with his solicitor. They asked me to obtain that. When I called up hi solicitor for his passport and visa, he added to surprise even more. He informed me that Dave's visa had been rejected in August 2004 only and he had informed that to Dave when he went there. He would be sending the rest of the documents by post. I was surprised as well as hurt. Dave had lied before me about his visa. He had kept me in darkness and the fear of getting betrayed again started groping my mind. I called up the home office too, and told them that his case was at Liverpool. The said that were not able to find any document in his name, and promised me to inform if they got something afterwards.

The day after he was arrested, two of my friends came to pay a visit to me and they told me that Dave had asked them not to tell me something. What they told me shook me completely. They had seen Dave with a customer at Hilton Hotel on Valentine's Day. I was at that time in Mauritius. He had already booked a table beforehand the bill of their dinner was 60 pounds per head. After that, he had also paid 425 pounds for champagne and twenty pounds as tips.

The day after they took him to prison, I went to see a solicitor on Friday who could be able to deal with his case. I still could not make my mind believe that he could have done all those. So, I started weeping before the solicitor and told him that Dave had been very nice to me and he was the loveliest husband in the world. My solicitor assured me on hearing those that nothing would happen to him, and everything would be fine. After coming back, I called up the police station and they told me that I could meet Dave next day that is, on Saturday.

My sister and brother-in-law had been helping me with the shop all along. I had to be very busy with my work. At the same, I was completely stressed out due to all these worries. I could not make out how to manage all the problems and expenses single-handedly. I felt I had lost everything and I had no one to support me. Next morning, I had my appointment at 1p.m. It was one and half hour journey by bus. All I way I kept on thing about how I would be confronting him. It was very, very hard for me to go to the prison and see him in that condition.

At last, the dreaded hour arrived. I was given two hours to spend with him. As soon as I saw him, I could make out that he was too stressed out. He was not the same person who used to dwell with me. Colour had drained from his life in these few days. On seeing me, he grabbed my hand and started crying bitterly. He was in his tears when he told me that he had not cheated upon me. He loved me too much and he just needed sometime to prove himself innocent. He told me that one day, I would surely know the truth and after that everything would be set right.

I was also sobbing and told him that I knew very well how much he loved me and I would be with him by his side all along the nightmare. I talked to him about our shop. He told me to take care of my health and the shop as well. He very well knew my characteristic of being fragile asked me to have control on myself and be strong, so that I turn out to be his iron lady. I promised to do so and after the meeting time was over, I did not have any wish to leave him alone. He had asked me to send his clothes, money for expense and his shoes. On the way back, I was feeling extremely lonely and was missing him by my side. From that day onwards, I used to go to meet him on every Monday, Wednesday and Saturday. I met him fourteen times per month. As he had told me, I sent him his clothes, shoes, 200 pounds for his expenses, writing pads, stamps etc.

It was very tough to lead my life that way. I was always out of this world in his thoughts. Moreover, our business was getting hampered due to him. We had lost many of our regular customers and I knew, I could not make in that way for long. I felt lonely while sleeping alone in the flat above our shop. I used to cry every day and recollect our sweet memories. He started calling me every night and talked to me every day. He would enquire about my health, and I always used to lie to him saying that I was very happy, and was taking full care of myself, never letting him know my actual plight.

As I was a woman, doing all these spontaneously was not easy and was tiring for me. I fell ill very soon and was admitted to a hospital for one week. As a consequence, I was not able to go to meet him or even call him in that condition. I knew that he had been feeling very bad and going mad due to that. Finally, being very impatient, one day he called up at the shop and my brother-in-law informed him about my condition and where I was. He was very worried and called at the hospital by taking permission at the prison. As I talked to him, I could feel his love for me and he told me that he would call me every evening and once I got well and return home, I should inform him at the earliest.

After the day I was discharged from the hospital, a customer came to meet me. I said ok to her and asked her to come to the kitchen. She told me that I was a very kind woman and she had no intention to hurt me, but she felt it was required to let me know that my husband had slept with her few times and had also paid her seventy, sixty and fifty pounds consecutively. But she assured me that Dave loved me from the core of his heart. It was just that he was a bit greedy. I asked her when they did that. She told me that it was in 2004 when our house was empty, and once when Dave had gone out of the shop giving the excuse to me that he was going to search a mechanic for our jeep. I asked her why they stopped that, and as a reply she told me that my brother came and started living with his family.

I made up my mind that I would no longer keep quiet and think about him. I should ask him about these ladies and would ask for an explanation. So, when in the evening, he called me up, I started to be rude with him and asked about those two ladies. He started shedding tears and acknowledged his guilt. He told me that he knew he had committed mistakes but I should forgive him. He was ready to fall at my feet for what he had done. He went on explaining that with the first lady, he just went out for dinner as she was single on Valentine's Day. She pleaded with him to go out with her as I was also not present. The second lady was in utter need of money and as she was desperate, he did sleep with her. I was quite angry with him and cut the line.

He had also cheated me. Moreover, he stabbed me on my back. My brain was being logical and telling me that he had done wrong and he must be punished, but my poor heart was still filled with love for him and asking me to forgive him. I went to sleep that again relying on the fact that night brings advice. The next day was a Sunday, and when called me, I showed my anger and did not talk to him. I also kept thinking all throughout the night whether to go to meet him or not. Next morning, I finally made the decision of going and when I reached there, I beg him to answer my questions honestly and truly. He told me that whatever I had heard about those two customers was true. He did not know how he did all those and after committing the mistakes, he felt grief stricken. He had thought that it was some mental problem and so he went to his G.P. and asked him for help. He loved me truly and his entire soul rested in me. He wanted us to have a happy married life, just I and him, and no one else. I was still doubtful so I asked him whether he was telling all those as he had no one else to support him. He broke down at my saying that and he told me that he loved me and I was his world. As long as I was there in the prison, I discussed about the problem with his behaviour and asked for some time to think over the matter.

After coming back, I was feeling very sick as well as tired, so I closed the shop. I tried to think that it was just a nightmare which had come to our life and would be ending soon. I was crying like anything and praying God to help me out. I did not know what type of life I was going to have and what my future held for me. I just prayed to God that I loved him so He must help me in taking a good decision. My heart told me that it is humans only who commit mistakes, and forgiving is a great virtue. If I had left him in that state, he would turn to be worse by getting frustrated. I was a good person at heart and made up my mind to help him as long as I could. I pledged that I would try to revive our good, old days and make him a better person. So, I continued to visit him regularly and performed my duties as well. I used to talk to him, give him support mentally by saying that I would be with him and he would be released from the jail at the earliest. I always used to think that God held me to be very courageous and that was why, he put before hurdles to test me, and I with his blessings would succeed surely.

Every day, I kept on praying God that once the case went to court, make some miracle took place and set everything right. I knew that he was my world and I could not imagine a life without him. I had started loving him even more instead of hating him after all these incidences. I tried to keep myself with my works in the shop as well as household works, but at night there was no rescue. As soon as I used to put my head on bed, thoughts regarding Dave came to my mind and I could not sleep. I was already almost dead with anxiety. I lost a lot of customers because of him and I started facing financial problems also, as I was not able to concentrate on my work properly and I was indebted to many people. Moreover, I had to go meet his solicitor every week. I was also getting older day by day, and it was getting difficult for me to bear so many things alone. At the end, I was so tired that I made up mind that let anything happen; after one month, I would be going to lead a quiet and peaceful life and devote sometime in healing my own future.

To be very honest and frank, I used to ponder about the reason behind so many sacrifices of mine for him. Why was I doing all those for him? When he did those unscrupulous things, I did not come to his mind even once and he had freely accomplished those. One day, I got a letter from my solicitor informing me that there was a hearing in the 3rd week of August, 2005. When I went to meet him, I could how eager he was to get release from the prison and come back home. He told me that he knew I loved him and did so much for him that he would remain indebted to me throughout his life. He assured me that once he came back home, from the very first day, he would be only mine and he would remain that for ever. I told him that I did not want a reward of his loyalty or slavery just for one day.

I made him understand that he was not obliging me. I wanted someone in my life who would love and care for me only. There was a few days left for him and I asked him to decide during that time whether he really loved me or not. If he did, he could come back to my life, else I did not need him. He was free to go anywhere or do anything. I had taken all these troubles for him because I loved him with all my heart and he must not think that he owed me. My love for him had made me sacrifice so much and visit him regularly to provide support to him. I did use to come to meet him, but I was not obliged or forced to do that. It was the love inside which asked me to do that. If he could love unconditionally without stabbing on my back, then only he could come back, else he could stay where he was and I would lead a life alone.

Hearing all these, he became very emotional and regretted his wrong doings. He told me that loved and promised that he would not be repeating such mistakes again. He need not think twice as he knew that I was his precious asset and he would never want to lose me. I had been his shadow all along, and everybody is aware of the fact that a body cannot live without its shadow. I was so proud and overwhelmed with joy to hear these loving words from him that they made me think, that when we would be retuning back to healthy lives, everybody would be envying us as we would be such a happy couple.

On the eve of hearing, I again went to visit him in the prison. I hoped for the best that I was seeing him in this condition for the last time. My heart was telling me that I would not be coming to the prison again. I had faith in two things, my God and my eternal love for him. The next day was a Tuesday, and the hearing was scheduled at 10a.m. So, I took my two friends along with me. As I was the witness of the case, I was not allowed to go inside and meet him. I stood outside. I could only see him when he came inside the court and I was standing in the witness box. Earlier, I had taken permission to assist the case. My heart was bleeding when I saw Dave handcuffed for the first time. I could feel from his face how he could be feeling.

Next day, I was so busy at the shop that I got no time to go to the court. But my mind and heart were at the court with him. The third day was the verdict day and I made sure that I had enough time after the shop to go to the court. When I arrived at the court, I was the only person sitting inside. At the very first, the judge announced the day to be the verdict day and informed that they did not know how long it would take, and once it was over, they would let us know. I kept on crying and shaking with fear all throughout the session. I could feel there was no one to hold my hand at this moment of crisis. I turned my back only to see Dave going along with the officers to the police station.

His barrister came to talk to me and asked me if I wanted coffee. I turned the offer down politely, as I was getting much tensed. It was already 45 minutes, I had been waiting since the judge had announced. I was getting impatient when the judge came inside and asked the jurors for their decision. There were twelve of them and the judge asked whether they found Dave guilty. I could not believe my luck when the verdict was finally out—it was eleven against twelve, not guilty! I was so overwhelmed with joy that I could not hold my tears back. I cried and cried, and let my tears flow. Dave was also crying. His barrister came to me and informed that I could take him home, but before that, we had to complete some paperwork and other formalities. He showed where to wait and I waited for 1 hour, though the time seemed to be never ending to me. At last, everything was done, and he was finally released. As soon as he was released, he came running to me and took me in his arms. He was getting extremely emotional and kept on complimenting me over and over again. He told me that I was his angel, God and treasure of his life. I could very well perceive his happiness and asked him to calm down and enjoy the first feelings of that long awaited freedom.

I called up my sister who had been helping all along in the shop in order to bestow upon her the good news that we had won the case. She congratulated me, and when we reached home, she was at the doorstep to greet us. She gave me a tight hug and told me that she had been much worried seeing my over confidence. Had something wrong happened, she was afraid that I would not be able to bear that. Everyone in the house was overjoyed on his return and he told me that he did not want to waste any time in relaxing. He said that he would be taking a bath, and after that he would help me in the shop. He asked my sister to take a day off as her kids were enjoying a holiday.

After he came to me in the shop, I was feeling at the ninth cloud, as I would not have to be alone now. We would again be together and work hard for clearing our debts. After we were done with the shop, he told me that the day was a special day, so it must be celebrated along with a special meal. I agreed with him and after having dinner that day, we decided that after that day onwards, we would not talk about the nightmare again. Later when it was time to go to bed, I told him honestly that it was not possible for me to sleep with them then only. I did love him but my mind could not make it up. He respected my feelings and said that he would never force me. He knew that it was difficult for me to accept the fact, even after I knew he was not guilty. So, we went to sleep separately that night.

Next morning, we woke up to the bright rays of the sun, and he held my hand, and said to me that it was going to be a new beginning for both of us. We made plans to renovate our shop again, and I went to the bank to take a loan. We were able to pay off the debts bit by bit. In two days, we had re-arranged our shop, and we tried our best to arrange for cigarettes and alcohol worth 3000 pounds.

LETTERS FROM DAVE: A SPECIAL COLLECTION

25/04/2005

I just want to say that I love you very much and that I'm missing you a lot. Believe me it's like being in hell having nightmares every night. Since you are so fragile, so vulnerable, please do take care of yourself. But by the grace of God, with your love and affection, we will come through. Hopefully, the storm will be over soon. I miss you and can't live without you. I do need you.

28/04/2005

Just to say I still and will always love and die for you. Be strong sweetheart.

29/04/2005

You said I have two faces—you neither have a heart, nor feelings. You said that I have been in your life just for your assets, and to act in your life. But I am really proud what you have done for me. I want nothing from your assets. I can't forgive myself, never ever, for what I have done to you. But if at all possible, give me a last chance. Human beings can make mistakes. If you feel that you don't love me and can't live with me, you have all the right to refuse me that chance. Never shall I complain or think wrongly of you. You are an angel as well as God for me. I shall never forget that. I know I don't deserve a good life after having done this to you. One day I shall die like a dog. You are my breath; you are my shadow, my life. I shall pray for you every time so that the Almighty blesses you. I shall write a book on your life and shall always keep it as a souvenir. I know you don't deserve the pain you have suffered. You are a very special person on this planet. There is nobody who will be like you. I love you so much.

23/05/2005

You said to me "Close your eyes and try to see how we were happy when we got married". It's true, we were extremely happy. Our world had completely changed. Never shall I forget the pain I have put you through. Believe me or not, I can't forget my stupidity, and the sins that I have committed. I shall pay one day for all that. I do love you and shall always do. I am really sorry for what i have done to you but I can't fix it. As I told you, it costs nothing to give another chance in life. You should just be strong and confident. Where there is a will, there is a way. In the future, my happiness will be with you, not without you.

I know I have a son who is secure with his mum. The only thing I need is you, your love as usual. Just give it a go, a chance, and you will see. It will be true love without ego. As you said the worst is done. Life owes you a lot so don't turn your back. I really love you and want to be with you forever.

Please forgive me, please give me a chance. Just one chance, give it a go. Life is beautiful; life is great, think, think positive. You are lovely, humble and great.

27/05/05

I can understand your feelings. I know you are still upset with me. I have been acting stupidly and obsessively. My stupidity

97

is the sole reason why I have been doing things I shouldn't have done. I have hurt you, your feelings, and have let down our love for each other. I am begging you for a chance to prove myself worthy of your trust. I don't want anything in this world except you—my love, forever and ever. Give me a chance to start afresh with you, leaving all sorry memories behind. That's the only reason I have asked you for the pads. I have started writing—yes I am writing a book on your life, the title will be "Fate" and I shall treasure the book until I die. I won't leave you ever.

16/06/05

I do apologise to you. I am very proud of my life; to have someone who loves me so much! I don't care about your age; people have no right to interfere in my life. I shall be with you till I die, that's a promise. I won't ever betray you or hurt you; instead I shall be by your side and love you more than ever. Together, we shall fight every problem that comes our way and build our lives. You are my heart-beat. How can I live without you? Our love for each other is very special. I was a monster, but now I have changed and become a human being. I am a new person—pure, honest, and faithful. My love is true and pure.

17/06/05

You are great, special, loving, caring and you are only mine.

20/06/05

Every time I see you on visit, I feel as if my love for you is growing. I know, rather I'm sure that the two of us, together, will beat every single problem in our lives. We shall always be optimistic and confident; we shall win every battle and soon be together. I shall make our dreams come true and live in a world without hypocrisies. At any cost, I won't let you down. I want to wake up every morning with you baby. I want to feel every beat of your heart. I want to be there whenever you need me. "Jaan", I love you more than anything else. I shall always be there for you.

21/06/05

I have loved you and shall always love you. I love you more and more every day, every minute, every second. Believe me, my heart beats just because of your devotion, your love. With your help and love, courage and devotion, we shall churn out a life for us that will be better than ever before.

I love you, I need you, I miss you, I want to be with you forever and ever. I want to be with you no matter what happens. I'll be there for you in the best and even the worst of times. I love you more and more. I'll love you till I die. I need you more than anything.

23/06/05

No need to think, I have made up my mind. I won't take a step back; I'll move ahead at all cost. I am confident in telling you that I have chosen to live with you till I die. Nobody can stop me. I and you will be a couple forever. You will remain what you are—my gorgeous wife and I have no regrets for choosing you as my wife. I am so proud of you today, that if one day, I hurt you, or betray you, I know full well that the world will be against me and God will never forgive me. You are my angel, my love, my wife, my saviour, and my God. I don't care about other people—I don't give a toss. I love you as you are and will always do so. It'll only be you and me, nobody else. Listen to your heart, and I am certain you will hear my name—the name of your love, your husband. Love never dies, it always blossoms.

Whatever the weather, summer or winter, I don't bother. Love is love, love is life. That's my message for you today.

26/06/05

Sorry love, I shouted on you when you came on the visit. Please try to understand, you have a lot to do with all these responsibilities, as do I. Please promise me that you will be calm and strong. I know you are a really nice person and all our problems have been stacked on to your shoulders. I'm here relaxing, and you have left to deal with all the problems. Darling, I pray to God to be with you very soon and to be able to pay you back, maybe even more than I need to. You are the only one in my heart; there's no place for anyone else. None can ever replace you. Our future will be fresh, honest, lovely and caring.

27/06/05

I know darling that all these problems that you face today are because of my big mistake, and I sincerely regret it. I have learnt a lesson. I love you very much and I'll do so for the rest of my life, hence, nobody will take your place in my life, in my heart, or in my mind. Only you will be there all the way through. I'm worth nothing without you. You are my life, my angel, my love, my breath.

It's only you and only you in my heart, mind, body and soul.

Today my heart is crying; I missed you so much, I can see how much you love me and what I have done to you. I know you have been looking after everybody in your life; you have never been selfish. I promise you my love—now it will be you and only you in my life and I'll make you the happiest wife on this planet.

I wish one day I could pay you back and reward you on behalf of everybody for what you have done in your life. I don't want money; I want your love, our happiness, and to make you the most wonderful person in this world. Money can't buy love—we both need love and with our faith, we will soon be together forever. Keep that spirit up. I promise you, today you are in problems, but in future, I won't let you down and prove to everybody that it's me who put you in this situation and it's me who is going to resurrect your life. We are going to rebuild our life; I'm not bothered about whether we stay here or in Mauritius. I'll always love you and be there for you all the time at any cost. You are my priority and that's final.

29/06/05

I know you are both mentally and physically strong. You are really great, greatest of all. You are simply the best. We can't stop loving each other. Just don't forget I love you very much. I miss you gorgeous. Just want to hold you tight forever and ever. I don't want to lose you at any cost. I want to be yours and yours only forever. Want to be with you for life. You are in every beat of my heart, in every breath I take.

30/06/05

Feel sorry for what I have put you through; you are great, you are my God. Be patient and soon we shall be together for a real, true and lovely life. Believe me, if you are confident, and keep your love and devotion towards me intact, we shall be successful in our lives. Today you mentioned that you don't want to think about your future but you will never leave me alone in my painful moments and will always be there to support me when I'm in trouble. I promise you that I've learnt my lesson and don't want to lose you. My happiness is with you my love; my future is with you, not without you. I am very proud to have a wife like you. You are always behind me and looking after me. You are the honey of my life, the juice of my veins. Every day, when you leave after the visit, I feel as if you have taken a piece of me.

You are my life, my happiness, you are my love, you are my desire; you are my sweetheart. God knows that's true. Nothing's going to change my love for you because I can't live without you.

03/07/05

Being in this place, I am stronger than ever, morally and physically. Don't worry in future I shall give you all the respect, honour, love and affection you deserve and nobody will ever take your place in my heart as well as my life and I shall be yours forever. Your age is just a problem maybe for the society; for me it's just a figure, nothing else. I still remember your last visit, how we both hugged each other, and cried. Don't worry, your Dave is strong and will fight till his death for his sweetheart—Pearl.

05/07/05

I remember what you told me—"When you are stressed, close your eyes, and think about me." That's what I did yesterday, and it was a very helpful experience. I just can't stop loving you. You are my love, my life. If you were not in my life, being in prison, I could end up dead, that's the truth. You are my heart, my soul, my love, my spirit, and the only reason, the only medicine for me.

07/07/05

Darling I love you. I don't tell you this out of gratitude for the help you have done, I really love you. It's just true love and I'll love you for eternity, whatever happens. Nobody can separate us. Age is not a problem. You know how much I love you; I shall be with you even when you are old. I don't care about anything. Believe me, I really love you and can't live without you. So how can I think of leaving you and living with someone else and start a fresh life? No way! We are made for each other.

08/07/05

This card is for the most beautiful, lovely, caring and dedicated wife.

13/07/05

Sweetheart, I know I made you suffer, I know your heart is bleeding, and it's all because of me. I promise you, I won't ever leave you in my life. Our love is so beautiful and strong that even evil has no power to destroy it. Trust me, soon we will be living a happy life together and everybody will envy us. My mum has given birth to me, but even she has not done for me what you have. As always, I would say that you are my world. I don't care about anything else. I just care for my lovely wife, Pearl. Love, I promise you, I am your property only, nobody else's—that's for sure. No more mistakes; I've learnt my lesson, even if in the hard way.

14/07/05

Thanks for everything; I am extremely happy and grateful to have a wife like you. Having made you suffer makes me feel guilty and degraded. When I put myself in your situation, I can see that I destroyed our happy life. There is no charge for love; the world is full of people who need someone who understands them. Keep smiling; you look great when you smile. I pray to God so that he helps us to rebuild our life, with love and happiness forever and ever.

18/07/05

Hope that God is happy now with our position, and soon will grant me my freedom and let me run to you and make you happy forever with all his blessings and protect us from every bad thing. I am impatient for that big day just like you are. The major sacrifices have all been done by you. I shall never forget that and that's why I ask God to let me be with you forever. I pray to him to protect us from evil and jealousy. I promised you that I won't let you be alone; if I do, God will never forgive me. You are my treasure, and I shall keep you happy till I die. No more tears in your eyes. Never again, since I just can't afford to hurt you again. Your feelings and love deserve special respect—I had that realization in the cell and I know now how much I need you in my life.

21/07/05

I know how you are dealing with your responsibilities. I know that you rush in spite of all difficulties to come for the visit. I wonder if I would have been able to make it if I was in your place. God bless you my love, you will be rewarded soon. I shall love and cherish you forever. I love you as you are. Thanks to you, I know what love means. It's a miracle how my life has changed since I met you. I love you darling. My love for you is deeper than the depths of an ocean.

22/07/05

I'm sending you a bunch of sweet and sour kisses, full of vitamins and love! Smile and be strong, my iron lady. You are mine only. I love you very much.

23/07/05

I can't wait to see you. I'll be there waiting eagerly. Pearl, let me tell you that it means a lot to me and I feel much obliged and would like to be thankful and grateful to you.

24/07/05

I don't know what is going to happen to me if one day you leave me. Being far from you, now I can feel the importance of your love in my life. Nobody can beat you, your love has got so much strength and purity in it that I believe you to be the WORLD'S NO.1 WIFE. You are an asset to me honey. I would like to share my thoughts with you; I want to tell you that you mean the world for me. Think of something you couldn't live without Dave and multiply it by 100, think of what happiness means to you . . . and add it to the feeling you get on the best days you've ever had . . . add up all your best feelings and take away all the rest . . . and what you are left with, is exactly how I feel about you. I really love you just too much. Love tugs heart—strings softly, sweetly and turns your life around completely. I want to tell you unlimited times that I do miss you. Whatever happens in life, I shall always love you and live for you.

Renooka Gopaul

26/07/05

You always say that you want a peaceful life, just me and you; and soon if God is with us, everything will be in our favour. I don't care even if you have to sell the shop or all your assets, I don't mind even you are penniless, I won't misguide you this time, I shall always love you and be there for you, rich or poor. I won't leave you, never ever. Even though I have been married to you, till now, I have done nothing for you yet, but I shall do everything I can for my lovely wife in future. Nobody can steal you from me. I shall fight till I die to win you. You are mine and only mine, I am so glad you are part of my life. I feel so privileged to be yours, and share myself with you, and walk together on the path that takes us in many directions. Sweetheart, you are the one who will make my life complete, more prosperous than I had ever dreamt.

27/07/05

Darling, I am here. I can't help you due to my own fault. I deserve to be punished but I feel extremely sorry for you. Because of me, you had to sell all your assets; never mind darling, my love will always be there for u throughout your life. It's a very hard decision but I am here for you and with two persons will power, he will be happy. Even if you have to go back home, we will. I just want to treasure my love, my wife, I want to be a good husband and do all my duties towards our life. Despite any calamities that come to our life, I know we will be the happiest couple on the planet. I shall leave everything for you; you are like a precious diamond in my life. I don't want to lose you. Keep your spirits high; we will succeed at the end.

28/07/05

I just want to say I love you. I am crazy for you; I am missing you a lot. Dave loves his darling Pearl, and he will forever.

106

Dave's life is Pearl, can't live without her. She is priceless and the most wonderful and most adorable wife ever, ever found on this planet.

29/07/05

I received my dad's letter today and he thanked you for everything you had done and are doing for me, for your devotion and for your concern about my case. You are an adorable person, staying by my side and fighting for me, that proves how special you are. I don't want to lose you at any cost. You are my most valuable asset.

30/07/05

I am happy to learn that you will wait for me whatever happens in our life. You are just too special, and I trust you sweetheart, don't forget I will be there for you whenever you need me. Hope that our bond remains intact forever and ever.

02/08/05

Pearl is Dave's soul, she is his heart. I don't care about anybody. All I need and want is your love and support. Hey sweetheart, you were looking really cute and cool in that dress.

08/08/05

Money is something we all need, but money can't buy you time, freedom and the most priceless thing in the world, the precious diamond which is known as love, yes love is the most valuable item in life and I am not prepared to lose my precious love. I mean it, because you are the most precious, most lovable, caring and devoted wife. Dave is madly in love with you. By loving you, I have experienced the happiness, pain, feeling forever and need to be with you and love you.

To me love means staying together forever; no one can ever take your place in my life.

08/08/05

Thanks a lot sweetheart. Even you are not well, yet you paid me a visit in the hospital which made me realise how much you care for me and love me, thanks a lot for your love, support and devotions. I pray to God that something wrong doesn't dominate my brain and don't hurt you. If a bee stings you, I shall suffer more than you; now try to understand how I feel for you. I shall never make you unhappy. God will never excuse me for that, trust me sweetheart, I have learnt my lesson in a hard way and for good reason you are my wife and I married you for eternity. I promise you that whenever you visit me, I feel so stupid, so naive, and so angry on myself, I can't describe the exact feelings, but I am really sorry for everything. I give you my assurance, that I would never ever forget this and this will be a challenge in my life. So that I'll never do anything like that anymore. You always say leave it to destiny, so be it. And if I become successful, I promise to give you more than you gave me.

09/08/05

Sweetheart, hope that everything will move in the right direction from now on. If I don't change even after all this, there is no place for me on this planet. Believe me or not, the love I have for you will change me. My mind will be clearer, and all my feelings will be purer. You will always be in my heart. I have lots of respect for you; enough is enough, no more tears in your eyes. A new leaf in the book of our lives is going to be turned. A new life will be ours, which will be full of love, affection, and honesty.

11/08/05

I am a new person now—clean and faithful. Trust me, I love you so much, if I do something wrong, God won't let me hurt a wonderful person like you. I'll never forget you; you are an angel for me. I shall give whatever you need—respect, love and maybe more forever. I have changed completely. I am your Dave, the Dave you want and love. I have learnt a lot in life; I know what pain, suffering, loneliness and separation feel like. I hope your God will help us and give me a chance so that I can love and cherish you and spend my whole life with you. I had entered your life came with problems, and have never done any justice to you. Hope that now all problems will be overcome and happiness will prevail.

13/08/05

You always say that you want to see me happy. My happiness is with my Pearl, nobody else. You are my shadow, and I can't live without you. I don't care about people. Our life will be shared just between me and you. Our love is so strong and true that none can harm us. Stop saying that I owe you—that's why I don't want to leave you; sweetheart, you are my love, I can't live without you. I really love you, and I know our love is very strong. I beg you; don't stop me from achieving my dreams, which is to rebuild our lives. It's about time you think for yourself now. You have done a lot for me and given me the chance to love and care about my sweet wife. You will be always in front of my eyes, my heart says I shall only be happy and find my smile with just one person who has sacrificed herself for me. And that person is my love, my wife, my angel, my darling Pearl. I love forever.

CHAPTER-11:
Hurdles After Hurdles

Everything else was fine, but it failed to cheat my eyes that our number of customers had constantly decreased after his return. But I kept my thoughts to myself only without letting him know anything. One day, I was talking to a good customer and she told me clearly that they not liking Dave to be in the shop. I understood that it was time for a change. I told Dave that it was time for his immigration and he must look for his passport. I called up at the Liverpool office regarding that matter and they said they would let me know in due course of time. I waited to hear from them for one week, but when they did not call up, I told Dave that was going to book a ticket for him to go to Mauritius. We would go there and look into the matter.

I booked the ticket for 26th of November, and faxed one copy of that to the immigration office. One day, when I went to the MP, they assured me that they would help me and would let me know. After two days, I got a phone call from them and they asked me to come. When I went there, the lady told me that at first, Dave was required to clear his visitor visa. After that, he would have to go back to Mauritius and apply for his spouse visa. They would be calling them up if there was any progress, as they were still trying to trace his passport.

Next day, he received a letter from the local police station informing him to go to sign at the local police station regularly on Tuesdays between 8 am to 12 pm. So, he started signing every week. I told him that we still had enough time in our hands to obtain his passport before his departure. In first week of November, he forgot to go to sign, so he called up the police station and assured them that he would go next week positively. When he went there the next Tuesday, he didn't return home even at 1 pm; so I called up at the police station, only to get shocked! He had been arrested and put in a cell, and was kept waiting for the immigration officer.

I rushed to see them at the office. It was nearly the closing time. All they did was to call up the immigration department at Liverpool and ask why he had been detained. It was conveyed to me that he had missed a signing on a particular Tuesday; so he had been detained. They told me to leave and call them the next day. After I came back, I went to the prison to meet him, and asked him if I was required to bring anything like his toothbrush, toothpaste, towel and other toiletries. He nodded in positive and I went back to home to get all those things. After that I came home very late. I was completely broken down by all these storms. I could bear them no longer. I did not have my dinner that night. I just cried and cried. I got frustrated with God and screamed to him questioning why it was me every time. What fault had I committed to be made to face such hard tests?

The next morning I hurried to the M.P. office and enquired about his detention. The lady there made a phone call to the immigration office and was informed that they had not been able to find Dave's passport and were yet to decide what action to take against him. I was quite upset, and they pacified me by saying that I must go home, and if there was anything new, they would let me know straight way. After coming back, I tried to call up Dave at the police station. They received the phone and told me that we had just few minutes. As I was talking to Dave, I broke down and told him not to worry, as I would be with him till my death. I said that my love for him was increasing day by day. He told me that he knew very well I would be with him forever.

111

That night, I prayed to God to impart me with inhuman strength, so that I could overcome these hurdles. I was crying in such a way that I was shedding all my tears in a single moment. I said to him that I had gone through two unsuccessful marriages, and in the third time, I was bit happy for the first time, and He had no right to snatch away even that from me. I wanted to survive on this beautiful planet, I wanted to live, and I needed Dave for that.

Next day, when the M.P. office called me up, I was so desperate that I started crying and could not say even a single word. They consoled me and asked me to come to the office so that they could have a discussion with me on what could be done. I went there and they informed me that that he was being sent to Manchester that evening. For that purpose, he would be sent to the Heathrow airport at 2:30 pm. They also advised me to try to book a seat on the same plane. I called up the Blackpool and told them that I had already booked his ticket on 26th of November which was the coming Friday. So, I requested them to let him stay for a week in Britain and then he would go back to Mauritius.

They turned down my request, and I asked them if the fare of the ticket which I had already booked could be utilized or not. I came back home and started thinking if I could book a ticket for myself in the same plane so that I was able to go with him. That way, Dave would be convinced that I loved him and cared for him. So, I managed to book a ticket for myself, and I called up the police station, and asked for permission to take a few clothes for Dave. They told me that I could take but I must carry just a handbag. After that, it was my turn to come back home and convince my sister that she would be able to manage the shop well without my co-operation. I encouraged her by saying that I was sure she would do well. Then I called up my friend and requested him to drop to Heathrow Airport on Friday afternoon by 5 o'clock. As I was living in Blackpool, it was almost three hours journey from there. He obliged and picked me up and we drove to the Airport. I had reached early and was waiting for Dave to turn up.

In the meantime, I received a call from Dave, and he said that he had called me in order to inform that he was going back to Mauritius. I replied back that his shadow was also accompanying him to Mauritius. He was happy for a moment, and then he became worried and said that he did not know what our fate held for us. I asked him not to be anxious at all when his shadow was with him, and told him that we would be meeting in the plane. I kept on waiting for him, when finally he turned up from my back and greeted me with a "Hello Darling"!

I told him while boarding the plane that he must relax as his shadow was with him and would be till her death. As the seat next to me was empty, he came and sat beside me and we started talking to our hearts' content. He told me that he knew that I would accompany him anywhere he went. He loved me and would never leave me. When the plane landed at Mauritius, it was announced that he would remain waiting for the cabin crew. He asked me to go and he would meet me afterwards. He told me not to worry, as his parents were informed about his arrival and they were at the airport. I continued to wait at the lounge but he did not turn up even after a long time. On the other hand, my relative was waiting for me at the airport. I could sense that something was surely wrong.

I did not want my relatives to know about anything, so I said that I was ready to go home. When I reached home, I told them that he had a problem with his visa and had to come back home to clear his entry and write a fresh application. He had to stay back to give a statement to the airport immigration officers. After about an hour, his parents came to inform me that Dave had been arrested because of the debt case. I was shocked and did not know what to do, as it was a Saturday. I told my sister that I was very tired after the journey and wanted to take rest. Actually, I wanted to stay alone and ponder over the matter in a cool brain. I must make out something. In the afternoon, Dave called me and told me that there was nothing to worry about and he would be coming for dinner. We had dinner, and after that he told me that he had to go to the court coming Monday, as they had taken away his passport, and when I paid the debts in 2004, the gentleman was required to give a statement on it. It was scheduled to be held on Monday, and he did not cancel as he wanted to clear all these problems at the earliest.

On Monday morning, he went to the court along with his parents. He was also required to find out that man. We went to the police a few times but they could not get hold of that man. He was fleeing away and he was doing it purposely. I had only two weeks in my hands, and so I was worried about our future. Already one week had passed, only to increase my tension even more. We decided to pay an amount to whoever helped us. At last, we did find a friend who agreed to help us with the matter.

We had so many commitments both at Mauritius and at England and we feared that we would not be able to keep them all. The friend did the work for us, but to our sheer bad luck, the work was accomplished on the eve of my departure. On the other hand, it would take about a fortnight to get back his passport. He was upset after learning that, but I consoled him by saying that I would be with him even after I went back. He calmed down, and next morning, I boarded the flight to London. It was Sunday morning when I reached London. It was almost 2p.m, when I finally reached Blackpool. I set to work immediately, cleaning my house and shop. I finished my work quickly and went to bed early that night. He called me up at night and we cried being emotional, because of the distance we had to face in our lives.

Next day, in the wee hours of the morning, at about 4a.m, I was waked up by a heavy sound. It was a bang on our shop door. When I looked from upstairs, I could see two people running towards a car. I was very frightened, and gave a call to Dave. He told me not to panic much and advised me to keep the shop closed. I hurriedly did that, and called up the police. After they arrived, they assured me that everything was fine, and there was just a deep scratch on the glazed door. It seemed that someone had hit it several times with a big hammer.

I was planning to keep the shop closed next day. I had to give an advance notice to my customers before doing that. It was required that I let the milkman, salesman too know about my plan. I called up a shutter company to arrange for shutters, so that our doors and windows of the shop remain thoroughly protected. I did that arrangement as I was going to holiday for one month as usual. I booked my ticket to Mauritius, and it was almost Christmas time when I reached there. Though we were able to recover his passport on 28th of December, we yet didn't receive his visa. It was told to us that nothing could be done before the beginning of New Year.

It was 4th of January, 2006, when we filled in the entire applications of obtaining his visa. We went to meet the high commissioner and we got an appointment with him in the coming week at 10a.m. we went on the scheduled day, and they interviewed him for a long time, and asked him to come back by 3p.m again. We went there, and finally succeeded in obtaining his visa. We were overjoyed at our success. I could not express my joy I was feeling in my heart. At last, we were destined to be happy after a long wait of four and half years. We planned to celebrate. We went for an outing and after that, we had lunch at a restaurant. We started planning exclusively for our future, and I dreamt of being us the most wonderful couple in this world. I thanked God for the umpteenth time for helping us again to recover our happy married life. We went back to England, and we did not open the shop on the very first day. Actually we could not do that as we had a lot of debts and bills pending, and our shop was also not arranged properly.

The very next day, he went to the authorities for obtaining his National Insurance number. They provided him with a provisional N.I. number and a letter by showing which he would be able to receive a job for the time being. Both of us started looking for a job, but at the end of the day, we had to be hopeless, as there were no vacancies. As I was qualified to get benefit till 2003, it became tough for us to make all the ends meet. I started filling up application forms for claiming and we had to make out in that meagre income only. But we found that we were happy with that. I realised that we need love in life for staying happy and not money. By the end of March that year, Dave was able to get a job of caretaker at a house, but by that time, we had already run out of resources fully.

I had a huge debt at the income tax office. They threatened me to sell off my shop so that they could get the money back. I wrote a letter to them informing that I would be selling off my shop myself very soon, and clear the debts. I did sell off the shop, took a loan on it and was able to pay the amount I owed to tax office along with the council tax on other properties. At the end, my solicitor handed me 4000 pounds back with which I decided to return to my old house at London. The other properties had already been seized by mortgage lenders. I was not at all aware of their fate. We came back to London, and I started bearing all the expenses until he was able to find a job.

As we had put our house at London on rent, we had to wait for two months so that the tenant had enough time in hands for shifting somewhere else. We had nowhere to go, and finally our luck survived when his friend allowed us to live at his house for those two months. By the end of July, the tenant had already left the house, and we could live there but it was in a very filthy condition. We started to clean the house as well as the garden and we were done after two months. Meanwhile, he got a job at a hospital shop which was having two shifts.

I had to go to Mauritius by the end of September. I was supposed to leave on 19th of September, and when the day arrived, he told me that he would go to leave me to airport. He asked me to get out early as there would be traffic jam. So, we did according to our plans, and we reached the airport five hours before my plane was destined to leave. After checking in, he kissed me and waved me goodbye as he had to go back to his workplace. His eyes were moist during the moment our departure and I warned him not to cheat again on my back. He would be a good fellow and keep distance from negative things. He assured me that his love for me was so deep that he would have to think twice before doing anything like that again.

On the day, I was supposed to come back; he was waiting for me at the airport to receive. No sooner we confronted each other, he was emotional and told me that he loved me and missed me all these days, even though I used to call him every day. When I reached home, I saw a welcome card and a big bouquet of flowers waiting for me. I was very happy to see those, and was assured that he did not do anything wrong on my back. I was relieved.

After a few days, I noticed that he was coming back home late by 1 or 2 hours. When I asked him the reason, he told me that it was due to heavy traffic on the roads, One day he came to me and said that he had found out an agency where he could work extra hours after his general shift. He wanted to do that as we were facing financial difficulties regarding paying the mortgage of our house. His general shift was from 6:30a.m to 2:30p.m, and if he worked overtime, He would be able to come back home by 6:30p.m. I told him not to take so much stress but he insisted on doing the job as he wanted to present me a happy and peaceful life.

Then one day again, he came to inform me that he was going to have a few extra hours at the restaurant of the shop. He would be starting the work at 8p.m and would continue till 10:30p.m. So he would come back to home by 11p.m, and it would not bother him from working in the shop in the morning. I told him that there was no need to go daily, and it would be fine if he went two or three times a week. He started that by the last week of September, and he went four times that week. I was not pleased at all and went to talk to him. I told him that and he assured me that he would do nothing against my wish. Moreover, he did not get any extra money at the end of the week. When I asked him, he told me that he would be receiving that after every fortnight.

On 1st of October, 2006, he came and told me that the friend of his whom I knew was going to celebrate his birthday on 5th of October, and he had invited Dave to a pub for the occasion. So, he went there at 8p.m. Though I was not quite happy with the invitation, I did not stop him from going because I thought he was working so hard, so he might get some relaxation. So, he went there on the scheduled day, and he called me up at 10:30p.m to inform me that he would be late in coming back home. I was not pleased. When it was 2a.m, and he still did not return, I got impatient and called him up. He told me that he was on his way. He returned home that night and did not say anything to me. He went to bed quietly.

Next day, he returned from work early, and he gave the excuse that he was too tired of doing extra hours. That day, I told him honestly and frankly that I did not trust him. So, he would not go out of the house at night any further. He was hurt and he told me that was honest, and he would introduce me to his friend's wife one day, and I may interrogate her about his honesty. I replied back that there was no need of that, as it was our personal life, and I would like to keep that to ourselves only.

After a few days, he came to me and told that he had got the job to sleep at a restaurant for one night as the workers had been to yard. I straight way turned him down, but he kept pleading with me over and over again. He convinced me by saying that they were going to pay him 100 pounds for one night, so it was profitable to work there instead of 3-4 hours at the shop. That was Saturday night, and in the morning, he came back home as his original shift was from Monday to Friday.

Sunday afternoon, he told me that he was again required to sleep that night as the person who was supposed to do the job had informed that he was sick. I was dead against that, but he told me that if he did that he would be able to tackle our financial problems. I still told him that he would not be able to go to his original shift if he finished his night shift only at 6a.m. But he assured me that he would be fine with that, as he was going to take his uniform along with him. He would have a shower there and continue to do his original shift. I could not say anything else; therefore, he went.

CHAPTER-12:

My Faith Raped Brutally

Next day, when he returned home, I told him that he would not do any more night shifts. He told me that it was not required anymore as workers were no longer working in the hospital yard. I heaved a deep sigh of relief. On Tuesday, he called me up and told me that he was required to help at the restaurant at night, as there was a doctor's party. He came back home at 3p.m and watched television with me a bit. When the clock stroked seven, he started getting ready, so that he was able to reach the restaurant by 8p.m. I called him in the midnight, and he said he was on the way. He returned home that night, he came back and told me that he was feeling too tired, and he would call his workplace and take leave giving the excuse of being sick. Next day, he said that he was going to meet an agency which would offer him jobs on the weekends only. When he came back and I enquired about the meeting, he told me that they had promised to contact him over phone and let him know the proceedings.

It was 15th of October, Saturday, when he came to me and told me that the agency had called him up and asked him to go to do a night shift at a warehouse that night. I was not at all pleased on hearing that and asked him to turn their offer down, as they had got no right to persuade someone to work like that. But he told me that he could not do that as it was his first day of job with them. He went there to work totally ignoring my words. That night, I requested my sister to come up to my place and sleep with me, and she kept my request. That night, we just ordered a pizza, and had dinner together.

He told me that he was fine with that, and he was going to take the rest of the food at his workplace.

At 12:30a.m, he called me up and told me that he was feeling very happy and light hearted after calling me. We talked for just two minutes, when he informed that his colleagues were waiting for him and he had to go. Next morning, he came back at 6:30a.m, and went to drop my sister. When we were having breakfast, he asked me if we could go for an outing. I refused him as I wanted him to take rest. He had been working in night shifts, even after he had promised me not to do that any further. So, he went to bed rather unwillingly. It was 1p.m when woke up jumping up from his bed, and regretted for sleeping so much since 9a.m.

He again requested me to go out as a nice weather was prevailing. So, we went out shopping. I went to the trial room to check fitting, and when I came out; I could see that he was messaging someone on his cell phone. When I asked him whom he was messaging, he told me that it was my sister. We came back home, and as usual, prepared dinner, had it together, and went to bathroom in turn. I went first. After I came out, I called him to go. He said that he would be going after sometime. I needed to use the hair dryer, so I went to the bedroom and saw his phone was on charge. I unplugged the charger, and saw that there was a SMS from Kevin on his phone.

I opened the message and was aghast to read the following. I was written, "Why you said thank you for last night, you didn't pay me. It was with love. I missed you a lot after yesterday night. Don't make me wait long". I stood there for some time motionless, trying to recover from the fact that I had been stabbed again at my back. I asked him from the bedroom who Kevin was. He was shocked and he came running to the room. He lied to me that it was his colleague. He had hurt me enough, so I asked him to go through the text which the so called Kevin had sent him. He looked at the content.

I could not hold myself anymore. My frustrated soul came out bursting. I started to swear, scream and shout at him. I asked how he could do the same thing to me again, even after I had loved him unconditionally and did so much for him. I told him that I could not carry on like that anymore, and would not live with him under the same roof. I snatched away the phone from his hands, and called the friend of his who had let us stay for two months at his house when we came here. I asked him if I could go over to his place and sleep over there. He said that there would not be any problem and if he could come to pick me up. I answered in affirmative. Dave sat on the bed speechless shedding his tears.

As his friend did not know anything of the argument between us, when he came to pick me up, he greeted Dave with a hello. He did not reply. When we went near the car, he asked if there was anything wrong as Dave had just burst out in his tears before him. When I reached over his place, I narrated the entire story to him. He tried to console me and asked me to calm down, but I was totally in a state of depression.

I tried to call back that number, and every time, it went to voice mailbox. So I sent the woman a text asking who she was, and the reason why she had slept with my husband, and how long they were having that affair. No one answered. Next day, I called her up in the wee hours of the morning, and she did receive the call. She told me that she was not aware of the fact that Dave was married, and saying that much, she switched off her mobile. I knew that Dave was having morning shift so I asked the friend again to drop me home. After returning, I just went to the guest room and locked myself. I cried uncontrollably on my luck. I did not know what I was going to do.

When Dave came back from his workplace, he knocked on the door and asked me to come out as he wanted to have a talk with me. At the same time, the phone in our lounge rang, and he went to answer it. It was brother-in-law calling from Mauritius regarding the 60th surprise birthday of his father which I had planned. He had been dealing with that over there. As only one week was left before we were scheduled to leave for Mauritius, he wanted to talk to me. So, I had to receive his call. While I was talking with him, Dave came and sat next to me. I told him over phone that I was going to cancel the birthday as I would give divorce to Dave soon. I complained that it was not possible to lead such a life, where I was not given any value and every time I was being stabbed on my back. He was shocked to hear that and requested me to pass the phone to Dave.

I gave it to him and I could see that he was talking to his brother in monosyllables. He was just answering yes or no, and tears were running down his cheeks. He told me that his brother wished to talk to him again, so I took the phone. His brother told me not to do that to them as his father was totally innocent and he did not know a bit of all those. His sister started pleading with me to forgive her brother for the last for her sake. She was telling sorry on his behalf and I should give Dave one last chance to rectify himself. I turned down her request saying that it was no longer possible. His brother again wanted to talk to him, so I handed over the phone to him and went upstairs. He could talk freely then.

When he had finished talking, he came upstairs and knelt down before me asking for forgiveness. He told me that he again committed the same mistake. He did not know what happened to his inner self at that time, and after everything got over, he used to regret over his folly. At about 7p.m, he told me that he was hungry as it had been 48 hours since we had anything. I was so hurt that I refused to do anything for

123

him cruelly. He started sobbing and told me that he loved and he was sorry for what he had done. His guilt feeling was killing him inside. When I looked at his eyes, I could see that they were really sorry. So, I decided to have pity on him.

I went to take a bath and went out for dinner at a restaurant. When the waiter arrived with the food, he took a spoon full of fried rice, and swore in the name of God that if he would commit any mistake again, God would surely punish him and make his food poisonous. He would not be in good health if once more he tried to cheat me. I was happy hearing those and thought he would be the best husband in the world. I had already suffered much for two days, so we vowed on 17th of October, 2006 that we would not think of the past anymore. We would live for the present and work hard for shaping our future well.

Dave even handed over his mobile to me. He said that he would be using my phone and if that lady called up again, I could talk to her and answer whatever I wanted. I came to know that he lady was 28 years old, and she was a Mauritian student. Her husband and baby had gone back to home, and she had been staying here for fourteen months. She was so desperate for sex that she approached Dave to help her in searching a boyfriend. When nothing could be arranged, Dave gave in before her as he had told her that his wife and kid were also at Mauritius, and here he was dwelling with his aunty. He meant me by that.

5th of October was her birthday only, and Dave had taken her to the same pub, where I and Dave too had our first date. Dave had never done any night shifts. He used to head to her place and they made love. She said sorry to me for all that, and told me that she would not have done that had she known about Dave's marriage with me. At the end of the month, when the bank's statement came, I could see that Dave had

1000 pounds on one credit card and had paid 75 pounds for drinks at a pub. When I asked Dave about that, he told me that neither of them, even the girl could not make love without a bottle of vodka. That was why, she had a huge debt.

CHAPTER-13:
My Efforts Continued

At the end of November, I and Dave went for the birthday party at Mauritius. We were pretending as if nothing had happened even after that great storm hit past my life. During that time, I met my step-son, Prince for the first time. He was the child from Dave's first wife and almost eleven years old then. I asked Dave to bring Prince at our place so that he spent a few days with us. One day Dave asked him his relation with me, and he answered simply that he was not aware of that. Dave told him that he was going to give him two and ask him again after that, so that he found out his answer. Prince said that it was fine with him.

Unfortunately after two days, Dave forgot to ask the question to Prince. So, on the eve of our departure, I myself took the initiative and went to Prince to ask him about my relation with him. I wanted to know if he had got the answer by the. He said that did not, and when I asked him again whether he knew about my relation with his Dad, he simply said no. On that day, I realised that he did not have any liking for me and he would never develop that.

When we came back to England, I narrated the entire conversation between me and Prince to Dave. He told me not to pay that much attention to his words, as he was only a kid. Even though I was not happy, I thought that Dave was perhaps right, and the attitude of Prince towards me would change in due course of time. In order to ease the situation, I started talking with Prince every time Dave called him. I also used to send him gifts on every occasion. I had the hope that one day he would like me even more than Dave. For me having a son was a special gift, and I tried to be his mom. But I was wrong in my thoughts.

In the middle of 2007, I was planning to go to Mauritius in January for celebrating my mom's eightieth birthday. A grand prayer was to be held on that occasion. I booked tickets for both me and Dave, and he applied for his permanent visa for UK in the home office. His visa was going to expire in November, so I called up the home in order to enquire about the details regarding renewal of visa. They told me that due to some problem, it was not possible for them to do anything then only. We were advised to take an appointment before 28 days of expiration date of visa.

At the end of November, 2007, Dave got an appointment to apply for his visa on 4th of January, 2008. They had informed us that there were two ways by which one can apply for visa. The first option was to send the premium by post; while the second one was to take an appointment at the home office, pay the premium there, and obtain the visa on that very day. As the second option was quicker, we opted for that one. We gave the premium, but the officer at the home office told us that Dave could not get his visa on that day, as there was some problem. So we waited till middle of January, but nothing happened. So, as my luck could have it, I had to go to Mauritius alone leaving Dave behind. His ticket fare was also wasted as that was not refundable.

It was required to be a couple for attending the prayers. That was why I could not attend that in absence of Dave. My sister and brother-in-law had to replace us. I was feeling very sad and unlucky. That was the second time we could not attend the prayers. I kept remembering Dave and my warning to him when I was leaving at the airport. I had again warned him not to do anything wrong. He had promised me to be good boy and he used to call me every day. The prayer continued for nine days, and when he called, I let him listen to the prayers. It was my belief that he had completely changed by that time.

Again Valentine's Day turned up that year, and when I returned to England on 16th of February, my Valentine's card and flowers were again waiting for me. Dave came to receive me at the airport, and said in childlike glee that he could swear of not doing anything wrong, and I enquire anyone regarding that.

Dave had to work in day as well as night shifts as he was working in the health care department of the hospital, and lots of workers were on holidays. He had to work in place of them. He used to show me all the rotas if he were working in any night shifts or extra hours. On 5th of March he came to tell me that he had to a course regarding his job at a University which was 35 minutes driving distance from our house. If he did that course, he would get a promotion, and thus his salary would increase and we would not have to face any more financial difficulties then. The classes were held on Wednesdays 9a.m to 5p.m. Sometimes, he used to go to night shift son Tuesdays and went straight to the University next morning instead of coming back home; he used to come back on Wednesday evening. He kept on giving me hope that he would get promotion and I would not require to worry the.

I started sensing some abnormality, when Dave started working seven days in a week. Fear again started probing my mind. I complained that he did not have any time to spend with me or take care of me. He was almost all the time outside the house. To that, he said that he was working hard just for our happiness and I had to understand that. I fired back that I needed not to understand anything, as I wanted happiness in life, and my happiness was with him and not money.

Dave was not at all happy with my words, but he promised to work less from next month. As the roster for that month was already prepared, he could not do anything at that time. Next day, the two of us went for shopping, and after we were done, he told me that he needed some money as he had to put fuel in our car. I was quite surprised as we had put petrol worth 80 pounds only last Tuesday, and how was it possible to finish completely only in a week. Dave was hurt and he said that our car had a problem, and he needed to fix that. Even that condition was such that our car might have to be sold. I asked him to sell off the car rather than spending money. Dave said that it was okay with him.

He spent 30 pounds on fuel again, and on that day I told him that from that onwards I was going to keep a watch on how many miles he was driving. After coming back home, I told him that I needed to talk to him regarding saving money. After six years of my marriage, I had decided to share the household expenses and I told him about that. He said that he would do according to my wish and went upstairs to sleep. He said he had done his friend's shifts in the last weekend, so on that day and next day, he would remain at off as his friend would be replacing him. We did not talk to each other that night anymore. I went to bed late as I wanted to witness Dave sleeping early.

Next morning, when we were having our breakfast I again reminded Dave of sharing our expenses. He nodded quietly in affirmative and said that he did not mind. But I was hurt, as even after being husband and wife, we had to live like partners. So I told him that if it was his wish, I would surely respect as I knew that Dave could not make all the ends meet with his salary. We did not talk to each other anymore that day. Next morning, at breakfast table Dave asked if I wanted to go for shopping. We also had to pay the bills. So, we went out and it was me who paid for everything we bought and even all the bills. Dave shared nothing in spite of promising that he would.

When we came back, Dave told me that it was not possible for him to make all the ends meet with his meagre salary. I said that I knew that. I went on saying that he was still my husband and I loved him very much. But it was time for him to work and bear the expenses. I wanted the position of a proper wife and I could not be bread earner anymore. I also could not help mentioning that I had done so much for him so long, and it was his turn then to return the favour.

I was already 55 years old that time so I said that I would not be able to work like before, and it was his responsibility to save money and bring his son, Prince to England anyhow. I would no longer be able to help him with his son as my life had already become hell with him. He responded by just saying that he was quite tired due to night shifts and went to sleep upstairs. It was 1p.m then. At about 5p.m, he called me upstairs and informed me that he had received a call from his friend and had to go to work one hour early for replacing his friend. I said okay.

When I went to the bedroom, I saw him getting ready to go to work. Though he had not worn his uniform, I did not say anything to him. He went out at 7p.m without bidding goodbye to me. I was surprised as well as hurt. It was the first he had done anything like that. According to his usual routine, he used to return back home by 8:15a.m. But next day morning, it was 8:30, and still he did not turn up. I had to go to drop my nephew to school at 8:30a.m, so I went out. When I came back at 9a.m, I saw he had returned but was upstairs. He came down and asked me if I had had my breakfast. When I said no, he just went to the kitchen and had a glass of water.

After that he told me that had to go to the surgery which was at 10 minutes walking distance from our house. HE did not return even when it was 1:15p.m. I called him and it went straight to voicemail. I left a message for him, and he replied that he would be bit late in returning home. When it was 5p.m, I called him up again and the case was the same. It went to voicemail. I sent him a message saying that I felt it was time to return back home. He did not reply. At 6:30p.m, I called again and it went to voice mailbox. I then sent him a message threatening him that if he did not return home or did not reply, I was going to inform the police.

After a few minutes, he called me and started crying. He told me that he loved me. He was hurt when I talked to him sternly regarding sharing the expenses, as I had never been rude to him nor argued with him. So, he was going back home. He would go away from my life and at that very time, he was at the airport waiting for his plane.

The very first that came to my mind and I asked him was about his passport. I also advised him to think twice before he left as I would not be able to help him to come back again. He said that he had already decided. Even though he loved me very much and was feeling extremely sad to leave me alone and go back, he could not help that, as he did not want to be a burden on me anymore. When I asked him about our car, he told me that his friend would drop it at our house. He was waiting in the lounge and was just about to board the plane. I could hear noise in the courtyard, when he ended the call and switched off his mobile.

I started weeping bitterly and cursed my own folly that I might have been wrong in behaving with him and I was paying for that. My sister came over my place that night for consoling me and stayed back. All my sisters as well as friends were trying to comfort me as much as they could. They advised me to call up his parents at Mauritius and inform them everything. But no one received the call as they were on holidays. Three f my friends stayed with me that night and we sent a lot of messages to Dave. His mailbox was full that night. So, I got tensed even more. By next morning, the mailbox was empty, so we again started sending messages. My friends were expressing their doubt that he might was still in England with some other woman. But I could not accept that as he did not carry any clothes with him.

That day, at night, my friend asked me if I knew in which department he had been working, so that they could call up there and enquire about him. I said that I knew nothing as Dave had not ever mentioned about that, but I just had the knowledge that it was some urology ward. So, we started calling up that ward, and finally at 11p.m that night, we got somebody in the concerned ward to talk to us. He informed my friend that Dave was on sick leave since last Monday and was to return next Monday, But he had not turn up. We, especially I was shocked to hear the truth. I had believed that he had gone to work that entire week. I had to accept the fact that he was again cheating with me. Whatever it was, I decide not to forgive him and play with my life anymore.

He was abusing my trust again and again. I realised that he had no true love for me; neither did he care for me. That night, my friend insisted on taking away the phone from me as if I had it with me, I would continue to send messages to Dave. They wanted me to sleep properly as I got very weak and was not keeping good health. I slept very soundly that night as I was very tired from the insomniac part I spent last

132

three nights. Next morning, when I woke up, I wanted my mobile back. When I switched it on, I could see a message from Dave. It said that he loved me dearly as he always had, and he had not done anything wrong. He was with his friend and he would call me later.

He called me after a few minutes and starting narrating the same story. When I rebuked him saying that I wanted the truth and he must tell that instead of fooling me, he told me that he did not like my sister staying with us. Once she was gone, he would return. He did not have any grudge towards me. He loved me and he knew that he owed me to a large extent. He wanted to stay in my life forever and very soon he would come back to my arms. I told him that I needed the car and he would leave the keys in the letterbox as I hated seeing his face. He said he would call in the afternoon again. I didn't reply anything back as I expected him to tell the truth at that time. I did not break before him the fact that I knew about his lie of going to work.

In the evening too, he talked casually with me as if nothing had happened. He told me that was missing me to which I said that he need not do that as I had not stopped him from coming to our own house. He said that he needed a break and would return in time. Next morning when I woke up, I saw the door keys of the car lying on the mat. Afterwards he called me and said that he bed ridden with flu. I kept mum. On Monday, he called again and said that he was going to come home on Tuesday morning. When he did not come on that day, I called him to ask where he was. He said that as he was late at his work and didn't have the car, he went over to his friend's place with him. He promised to return on Wednesday morning.

Next morning, he informed me over phone that he would be late in reaching home as he had to attend a seminar. He also said that he had lost his phone and he was calling from his friend's phone. So he would not be able to call me anymore after that. Once he bought a new phone, he would let me know. I had a feeling that he was trying to avoid me. He didn't have a phone meant I could not contact him. I could know where he was and what he was doing. I tried to call the hospital ward and they informed that Dave was on off last night. In the afternoon, I planned to go to the hospital to enquire about him. I went to my friend's place and narrated everything to her. I begged my friends to let me go and asked them to accompany me to the hospital. When we reached there, I asked them to wait at the car parking area while I went inside and met Dave.

At last I got the ward which I was searching and went towards the closed door. I called them and said that I was Dave's wife and I wanted to meet him. He received the phone and asked me to come inside the staff room. I asked him again to tell the truth. He said that his phone was lost. Meanwhile, I noticed that he was not wearing his wedding ring. When I asked him about that, he told me that he had forgotten it at home. I was angry and asked him not to fool me as I was his wife. By then, I had also informed that I knew about his sick leave last week and so, it was better for him to speak out truly. I threatened him that I would not move even an inch without knowing the actual matter. I was his wife by the name of God and I had every right to know the truth. He kept quiet for a long time listening to my words.

At that time, my phone started ringing. I saw the screen; it was my sister who was calling me to come back. I told her to leave with the car and I would get myself a cab for going back home. She kept on insisting that she was not going to leave me with Dave alone. I said okay and asked her to call the cops if I didn't return by midnight. Dave was quietly listening to everything I said. My anger grew and patience was gone with his constant silence, and I started screaming and swearing at him. I reminded him of all the sacrifices I did for him and said that he was ungrateful who had forgotten everything. At 11p.m, he opened his mouth and asked me to wait for 5 minutes.

He came back and asked me to follow him. When we were out of the hospital, he was pursuing to the car parking area. I was amazed at his action as I was wondering that if he didn't have a car then why he was going there. A bigger surprise welcomed me when he took me to a very nice car, which was registered in 2005. He opened the door of the car and asked me to get inside. On the way, we didn't talk to each other at all. I kept on thinking whom he was living with and whose car he was using. Finally he took me to a house which was only at 15 minutes walking distance from ours.

It was a rented house and he had rented a room upstairs. The landlord came to talk to Dave at the entrance. We entered the room and to my shock there were many bin bags full of his clothes. I never knew of those. I could sense that there was someone else living in the room. I started searching the wardrobes if I could get anything. I found a receipt from Tesco dated 5th April, Saturday worth 105 pounds. It was paid by a credit card for buying bed sheets, duvets, two balance sheets and toiletries. She also found another receipt from the landlord dated 6th April Sunday worth 405 pounds. The payment was done in cash for depositing the rent of the house and a week in advance.

I asked Dave how he could manage to do all those as we were having a hard time in paying the 1200 pounds as rent for our house only. Other than that, we also had to pay his debts as well as other expenses. He said that he again committed mistakes and he was sorry for that. Next Sunday, as my sister would be leaving he would come back home. He told

135

me that he had not shown his lewd character anymore and so I should be relieved, forget everything and forgive him. I was extremely upset with his actions that day and my frustration level reached its height. I asked how many more mistakes he was going to do and I had to suffer because of them.

He again promised that he would not any more mistakes. He also promised to come back the next day and help me in cleaning the house and the garden. He came that day, and on Saturday, after his work was over, he started to pack his clothes so that he could come back to his so called sweet home on Sunday. Though six years had passed since our marriage, it seemed to me as it had happened just yesterday. We stepped into the seventh year of our marriage, and I again started hoping that everything would be set right in that year, as it is believed that number 7 brings luck.

CHAPTER-14:
Hopes Shattered Again And Again

Dave came to drop me home after that incident and before leaving he said that his heart was bleeding because of parting from me. He promised me to come back next day, and said that he had not had a proper meal since a long time. I took pity on him and said that I would cook for him and we could have our dinner together at his place. When I asked him to come and pick me, he told me that his landlord had prohibited the entry of any woman in his bedroom. So, he needed to have a word with his landlord before taking me there.

At 6:30p.m, I had completed preparing the dinner so I headed over to his place. We had dinner together, spent one hour and I came back to my home. On Sunday morning, he called me to enquire if I wanted to go for shopping. He would come and take me. So we went for shopping and he dropped me home at 12 noon. He said that he would be back after 4pm.m when my sister would leave. At 2p.m, he again called me up to inform that he was waiting at the supermarket car parking area and I should inform him as soon as my sister left. He also said that he had committed mistake for the last time in his life and he would not do anything further. I could be sure that there was no woman in his life that time.

When he came back that afternoon, he asked me to forget the past so that we could start a new life together. He assured me again and again that he was not with any woman that time. When I asked for an explanation why he was on sick leave for one week he told me that stayed at house only on Monday and

Tuesday. He went out with his mates on Wednesday, and as they got late, he stayed over his friend's place that night. After that he could not return home as he was feeling guilty as he had hurt me.

He told me that from that day onwards, we were going to lead a happy life, as since he came to my life I just had to face problems. He would not let me suffer any more and the next day would be a new day as well as a new beginning for us. We decided to plan together so that our wedding worked. He promised me to call during the break hours every day. Even I was free to call him at his ward whenever I wanted. He would not do any more night shifts from then and concentrate more on shaping our family. I was going to be the one and only woman in his life and the world would get envious on seeing a happy couple like us. To be very honest, I was not hundred per cent sure and could not trust him fully. But whenever he talked to me like that, the soft corner for him in my heart persuaded me to believe him and so we started the journey of life.

After a few days, he came to me and said that he wanted to confess something. He told me that there was the existence of another woman in his life and he started the affair with her when I went to Mauritius for the prayers. He had met her at the hospital as she was too working in another hospital along with some agency. She was from Gujarat and her name was Laka. As she was divorced with two daughters aged 17 and 15, and she herself was 45 years old, it was not easy for her to find out a boyfriend. So, she came to Dave for help. She didn't want any commitment; she just wanted Dave to take her out twice a week and had sex. He did not try to cheat with me but he failed every time. He doubted that he was having some problem with his behaviour and he would consult a GP. Dave was remorseful for having that affair and as he had promised me to be a good husband, he felt he would confess everything.

But he had ended all relation with her and there was no one else in his life other than me.

That day I cried like anything. I could not imagine how he could do that to me so many times. I had lost all my assets because of him. I was 55 years old and not keeping a good health. My friends and many relatives broke up with me, and I let them go because I wanted to be with him. And what he gave in return? He had let me down and made me feel so small in front of all of them. I had a belief that I would someone by my side to support me. But I had lost that. I had a hope that h would love and care for me after I had suffered so much with my past husbands. But he poured water on my faith. I prayed to God earnestly to provide me with enough courage to fight with the reality.

I could not hold back my tears and I went on telling him that He didn't know how much I loved him and I didn't even know what relation I bore with him. Every time he used to back stab me and my brain told me not to forgive him. But my poor heart would not listen and persuaded me to forgive him. So, I continued living with him but I was not able to lead a normal anymore. Though my heart used to say that he would return the same love to me one day, whenever I was in bed all the incidents of cheating flashed before my mind, and I used to get depressed. I was very frustrated as my life with him turned out to be hell instead of heaven which I had expected from him from the very first day of our marriage.

One day Dave came and informed me that he would not come back home during his break time that night as he and one of his friend had planned to go out for dinner and they were going to order a take away. My intuition told me that something was wrong, so I called him up in the ward and he answered back. I thought that maybe I was wrong. He used to call me often from his workplace so that I did not need to call him. I started regaining the trust on him back. One night before leaving he asked not to wait for him, as he was not coming for dinner as he would be very late. But he did not return at that night. He gave the excuse that he was extremely busy with his work. These few days, I felt very lonely and could not sleep at all at night. I tried to watch T.V. and divert my mind from him.

On 17th of June, Sunday, he came back home and told me that he had to go for a training at the University on 19th of June that was, on Tuesday. He had night shift on Monday so he would be going to the University directly from his workplace instead of coming back home. I was not happy and told him that they had no right to make him work more than 12 hours in a row and he would get Monday off. He promised me to talk to his manageress, but I reminded him that the manageress didn't come to office in the weekends. He said that he would call her up. Monday morning, before returning home, he called me and said that called his manageress but she could not grant him off on Monday night, rather she granted two nights off on Tuesday and Wednesday. I was displeased and asked him to take help of the law as it was against the law to make someone work for than 12 hours in a row, and the person would get 10 hours rest. Dave told me that there was no need of that. He even said that I was very stupid and I was not aware of the modern day laws regarding work hours.

So he went on Monday night, and he called me at 10:30p.m and told me that there was shortage of staff and they were really very busy. He wanted to leave everything and come right to me. He again called at 11:30p.m and informed me that he might not turn up for dinner at breakfast, as the site manager had arrived and he needed help in showing him around. If Dave could arrange someone from the agency, he would come and asked me to wait for him till 12:30a.m, and if he did not return by that time, I should understand that he was very busy with his work. I waited for him till 1a.m, and then I called him up. But the call went straight to voicemail.

I was worried so I called up at the ward and to my shock, they told me that Dave was on leave and he was supposed to resume his work on Thursday. I was going mad at Dave and did not know what to do. I understood very clearly that he was up to something wrong. He was never going to change. He would continue to commit his stupid mistakes and ask for forgiveness afterwards. I was unable to bear and I prayed to God to provide me with enough courage before it was too late. I could not sleep that night and waited impatiently for sunrise so that I could seek someone's help.

In the morning, I again tried to call him a few more times but all those went to voicemail. At last, I sent him a message at 2:30p.m which said that I had called the home office and asked them to return the visa application. At 4p.m, he called me and asked if I was at home. He would be coming. I asked him where he had been all night and he asked me not worry. He was going to tell me everything after he returned.

At 5:30p.m again, he called me and asked to come back home as he was not able to open the door himself. I was not very far away. In fact I was hiding nearby, and was keeping a watch on his actions. He could not open the door as I had left the door keys inside the keyhole. So, I came through the garden door and opened the door for him. When I asked him for an explanation he started crying and asked for a final chance. He told me that he was sick; he was really sick mentally. But I did not melt that time and asked him to pack his belongings and get out of my house, as he was no longer the person with whom I wanted to spend my entire life.

He started shedding his crocodile tears and told me that he loved me and did not want to leave me. I must forgive and be by his side and help him to change. But I was so fed up with all those that I started screaming and said that I was not going to give him another chance. He had to leave. I did the thing which

I had never done in my life. I started hitting him with my hands. He went upstairs sobbing and started packing his bags.

After he was done, he came downstairs with two bin bags and knelt down before me. He appeared to be emotional and told me that I needed not to be sorry as I hit him. He deserved that. It was the right thing for him. His parents would have given that punishment to him earlier, but as they didn't, he turned for the worse. It was like a wonderful gift which I gave him. He could come up to my expectations even after he had given me so many hopes. So if I wanted him to go, he would leave. Before leaving, he wanted just one promise from me. I should bring his son and look after him after he passed away. He said that he was going to commit suicide.

I kept mum instead of reacting. I looked at him silently crying and lamenting. And I don't know, what happened to me that day which provoked me to forgive him. I was again melted by his tears which made me even say that we would be thinking about the issue of his soon. I told him that we were going to live under the same roof as husband and wife, but it was not possible for me to sleep with him on the same bed. I could not do that and I needed a break. He said that he was not going to force me and would not do anything against my will. He would give me time to recover and after that, he was going to narrate the entire story to me.

He said that he was going to send a message to that lady telling her sternly that he would no longer be her sex slave. If she still required an escort, he would book for one. He didn't want dogs in our lives. He also said that from then he would work for just 37:5 hours per week. He would stop attending to any more courses at the University. Rather he would concentrate on his family and give me a happy life. He would prove that he loved me whole heartedly. Even after so many promises made, it was almost impossible for me to bear the previous facts. My life started getting worse. He wounded my mind and it was so deep that I required two weeks to recover a bit. Even after that, I felt like running away from the house and taking a break. Sometimes, I could not even talk to him properly.

I finally told him that I really needed a break. In fact I lied to him. I could not say him that at times; I could not bear seeing his face. He said that he understood my problem and he said that he was going to change his phone number, so that no one could contact him. He also planned for a holiday next week at Ireland. He had booked rooms for us in a four star hotel, but didn't plan for any outing. He said that it was going to be according to my wish after we reached there. He told me that he was sure that I would feel better after retuning. It would bring us closer. He would be the best husband and one day, he would give me more than I had done for him. I was happy listening to all those, and felt again that we could be the best couple. In our world, there would be just he and me, and no one else. I dreamt of living a new life in a new life aloof from the rest of the world. The holiday was short so I did not have a nice time there. I felt it could have been longer.

It was almost the end of July. He used to call me often from his work and ask me if I was okay. I laughed and told him not to worry as I was his iron lady. During that time only, he met a friend, and that friend of his gave him an offer to work as a caretaker at a home. He came and asked me if he can accept that, as he was working for just 37:5 hours, so he would work more and earn more so that we could have more holidays together. I asked him if I could trust him, as every time he used to join a new job, he was sure to have an illicit affair. He tapped on my back and said not to worry. It was going to be different that time, as earlier he was a dog but he had transformed into a human being. All that he wanted was a happy life with me. He would be happy if I trusted him and let him go.

I was still not getting confidence and said that he could go if he wanted that at any cost. So he went to have a word with them and started working from the end of August. He even brought a list of his working days and working hours and asked me to keep track of the wages he would get at the end of the month. He did not have any more night shifts. He used to be at home after his normal shifts and I was happy with that. He even handed over the exact amount of wage according to his working hours at the end of September. He became loving and caring as before and often asked if I still doubted him. I said that I didn't and he was happy too.

One day in October, he came and told me that they were giving him extra hours and night shifts, and he would do that for earning more. I grew suspicious again and asked him whether he was speaking truth and they were really giving him night shifts. He asked me not to doubt him and help him forget his past. He would show me the wages according to his working hours at the end of the month. I said okay. So he started working in night shifts but not daily. On the last Saturday of October, he went to work in his original shift from 8q.m to 8p.m. At 3p.m, he called me and said that he was going to do night shift as well as the person having night shift had informed that he was sick. I told him that they could not make him work more than 12 hours.

He said that it was not a problem for him as he would be able to sleep at night as it was a light duty. As he was already booked for Sunday morning too, it meant he would have to work for 36 hours continuously. I was severely against that and asked him to come back. He told me that as he would be working on Sunday, which is a holiday, they were going to pay him more. So he would have a huge income. I cut him in the middle saying that I didn't need more money. Rather I need him, his love and company. He told me that his manager had already left and therefore, it was not possible for him to do anything then. I was angry and asked if he wanted to kill himself.

At night, I could not sleep. I felt like crying and it seemed that my heart would explode. So I called him at 1:30a.m and when he answered I could hear the sound of cars in the background. I asked him if he was really at work. He was hurt and told me not be so suspicious about him. As they were sleeping inside, he had to come out so that he could reply. That was why I could hear the sound of cars. I was bit relieved. Next morning, he called me a few times from work to enquire if I was okay. When he came back on Sunday night at 8:30p.m, he didn't look even a bit tired. So I asked him if he was really at work. He told me he was and asked me to check his wage when he would get that. At the end of October, when he gave me his wage, it was just the half of the working hours. When I asked for an explanation, he said that he had to talk with his manager regarding that. Next day, he came back and said that his manager was on holiday, and he would enquire as soon as he returned. He continued doing more extra hours, not at night, but during the day only. The case was the same at the end of November too. His wages were half.

When I got surprised that time, he told me not to worry. He would not let them go off anymore. He would ask for his money straightway. If they refused to give him, he would stop working there. He knew that it was natural for me to get suspicious, but I should not as he was trying his level best to change into a better person. He would live happily with me and return back whatever I deserved.

In the middle of December, one day he came from work and went to rest. He said that he was not feeling well so he went to his GP and he had advised him to take rest for a few days. He took sick leave from the hospital but he continued going to do the job of caretaker. At the end of December, he came and handed over 600 pounds to me and said that it was the pending payment of October. The rest they were going to give him at the end of January. I was happy. He said that as they had paid him, he could not stop working. He was getting his flat pay at the hospital so by working there; he would have an extra income which would help us to lead a better life.

ON 5th of January, 2009, he came back from work at 8:30a.m. After having breakfast, he went to sleep. He woke up at 5p.m and saw that it was snowing outside. So, he said that he was required to clean the car. And when he went outside, he could not find the car there. He came inside and asked whether I had seen or kept the car keys. At last, he rang the police and gave a declaration that he had lost the car. He was quite sad due to that. Next day, he called at his workplace and informed that he would not be able to go to work because of that incident.

Next day, we had an appointment with the solicitor regarding his visa. I asked him not to worry much and assured him that God would help us in paying off our debts. He also had a loan of 13,000 pounds on the car. We went to the solicitor and he asked for a fee of 3500 pounds. He told us to give half the amount in advance so that he could start preparing the papers. We told him that we would let him know the next as we knew that we didn't have that much money with us. We came back and I started thinking about what we could do. At last, I decided to borrow some money from my sisters and give it to the solicitor. So I did according to my plan. I gave half amount to the solicitor and told him that I was going to pay the rest in three instalments.

When we came back home, he held my hand s and said that he did not understand my feelings for him. He was a moron who didn't realise my love and that was why he had hurt me so many times. He said that he was extremely sorry for the huge debt as well as the car. I asked him not to be sorry as I myself was not so happy with the car. It was better gone. The souvenirs in the car were also not good. I told him honestly that though that was a nice car, I did not like it from the very first day as he had bought that for Laka. He cried and said that I was no less than an Angel for him and sometimes, he felt like praying to me rather than to God. My eyes became moist. I could feel his tears on my hands, and I told him to change his bad manners and live with me happily. We would be the happiest couple and there would be a lot of people who would envy our happiness. I assured him that every bad memory would be forgotten soon and we should keep our fingers crossed. God would surely help us in obtaining his visa.

From that day onwards, he started travelling by bus. He used to come back and complain every day that he was getting tired of traveling two hours by bus. I asked him to be reasonable and said that we could not afford anything better. But soon we would buy a second hand car. One day I was going through the local newspaper and my eyes fell on an advertisement which said that a place was required for foreign students for 2, 3 or 4 nights. I gave that a try and did that for 6 months. I was happy as I had saved enough for our holidays. I kept that sum aside as I didn't want to spend that.

On the 5th of February, he woke up at 5p.m and came downstairs. I was watching T.V. and he sat beside me. At 6p.m he said that he was going to take a shower and get ready to go to work. His phone was left on the bed, and when he was gone a message came on his cell. It was from Laka. It said that she had given him her daughter Sania's new number and he would save that. I was mad with anger and I went upstairs and started banging on the bathroom door asking him to come out. He came out and I showed him the message and started shouting. I wanted an explanation. He told me that he was not cheating on me anymore and he didn't know why she wanted to give her the new number. If I wanted, he would talk to her in front of me only.

I called in the two numbers and no one received the calls. So I called in her daughter's number and she received. I said to her sternly if she knew me. I introduced myself as Dave's wife. She fired back that Dave was not married. I told her that I already knew about their affair and she had slept with my husband. She was still in her fierce mood. She threatened me that she could call the police and sent me back to Mauritius as I was not a citizen of England. Saying so, she hung up.

I turned back to Dave and said to him that I wanted the truth. He had to speak out. I asked not to go to work that day as I wanted an end to all those drama. I had never stopped him from going to work as I knew the importance of work in his life and that also, in a foreign country. First he called his office and informed that he could not go that day. Then I asked him to call Laka and tell her that I was a British citizen and I could complain against her if I wanted. If he really didn't had any relation with her, he would call her and made it clear to her that he was married happily and she would never bother us by calling anymore. He called her and sent a message to her asking her not to disturb us anymore as he loved his wife.

On that day only, he told me that he loved me and he had been faithful with me since June 2008. He didn't do anything from that time and I should believe him. He left all his bank cards with me. He didn't have any money with him and whenever he needed money, he used to ask me for that. I started believing that he would not do anything wrong as he had no money with him. He wanted me to do all the expenses as he wanted to save money for bringing his son to England. I agreed to do that.

By the end of March, 2009, he got the permission to stay for indefinite period in England. We started planning and saving for our future. At first, I paid off the money that I borrowed from my sisters with the help of the amount I had earned with the students. The rest we used in planning a holiday for that year. At the end of April, we started thinking to bring Prince to England. So I called the home office and asked them what to do. The marriage of Dave's brother was fixed at the end of August. So we booked two tickets at the end of May for going to Mauritius. When we were in Mauritius, we had already applied for Prince to the high commission.

When we came back to England, I knew that we had to be patient as the process was not easy. Nothing was done for a long time. He used to worry a lot about our future. I assured him every day that everything would be fair and we would be a complete as well as happy family. At the end of September, Dave called the high commission at Mauritius and they asked him to go over there. We didn't have enough money to pay the fare. But I asked him not to worry as I had some savings and he also borrowed 500 pounds from his friend, and we were able to pay the ticket fare.

CHAPTER-15:
A New Compromise

Dave went to Mauritius for 15 days. He was quite excited about his son. Even I was excited as well as happy with the thought that I was going to have a child at last. Dave called me and said that everything would be soon fixed right and they both would be arriving at the earliest. So, I started redecorating my house, and I furnished one of the rooms in such a way so that it looked like a child's room. I bought lots of new things and toys for him to make him happy. I bought a new mobile for him too even though I had already gifted another two before.

On 3rd of November, Dave called me up at 7 am and asked me to fax my visa, bank statements and all other important documents. I had to do it by 10a.m so I started looking for the papers and went to a shop at 9a.m for faxing them. I was very scared with the thought that if anything wrong would happen, he would be very upset. Before faxing them, I made a small request to the immigration officer that I would be very happy to get a son at that age, and it would be very kind of him if he granted Prince's visa. But as our fate could have it, the officer was engaged in a meeting at that time, and the office used to close by 3p.m. So he did not get my request and they did not grant Prince the visa. So, next day, Dave had to come back alone.

Next day, Dave got a phone call from his parents. They informed him that Prince was granted his visa and he was excited with the idea of coming to England. They wanted to know when they could send them. I told them that 9th of November, 2009,

Saturday would be fine. We both decided to go to the airport to receive him. His dad was extremely happy to see him. When we came back, Dave showed Prince his room. On that day I was so happy that I had invited all my sisters and nephews for dinner over my place so that Prince didn't feel lonely. Even my nephew, who was the same age as Prince agreed to stay overnight to provide him company. Next day his dad went to work early at 7a.m and he woke up at 11a.m. I made his breakfast and showed him how to do that as in England, everybody was supposed to be independent and do their own work. He did not even know how to use kettle, but I assured him that I would always be there to help him with whatever he wanted.

Later, I asked my nephew to set the mobile phone for him. When my nephew was gone, Prince came and asked me if he could use my laptop for checking his mails. I was quite surprised as I had not expected that a little boy like him could have mails. In Mauritius, computer possessing individuals are rare and that too, at the age of thirteen. I gave him laptop at 4p.m and he used it till 9:30p.m. His dad returned by that time and he switched off the laptop and left it on the table. I told him that I did not use to give my laptop to anyone not even to his dad, so I could not give that to him frequently, but he could have that sometimes.

Next day, Dave called me from his workplace and asked me to give my laptop to Prince as he needed to register for a voucher for his phone. I stood with my jaws apart. I could not make out why Prince himself didn't ask for the laptop if he needed that. I felt that I had to give him some time to become friendly. I gave him the laptop and asked him if he needed any help. He said that he was able to do it. Even after two hours he was not done and kept on running upstairs and downstairs restlessly. I asked him if he was looking for something. He said that they were asking for a reference a number and he was not able to do that. So, I said that I was coming for his help.

151

I went to him and checked on the computer screen. It said that he would receive a message from a particular and the reference number was given there. I showed him on the phone and told him what to do. After that I opened his inbox but was surprised to see it empty. So I asked him where the message was and he said that he had deleted that. I wanted to know why he did that and he simply told me that he wanted to. I was taken aback by his rudeness, and said that his dad was going to help him after he returned. I turned by back and went away.

When his dad returned from work at 9:30p.m, he switched off the laptop and left it on the table. Next day, when I turned on my laptop I was greatly surprised to see that Prince had registered himself in quite a few websites. I could not make out how he could know about all those at such a tender age. I was sure that even his dad was not aware of those. In fact they were nothing good or useful. They were the adult websites. So I told Prince that I was not going to give my laptop to him anymore. I must be careful.

Next day, I went out and his dad was with him. When I came back, Dave told me that Prince had called up the customer care and registered for his voucher. I did not believe that and said that it must be Dave who did that. He told me to believe that it was done by Prince and asked me why I did not believe him. I said that at the first go; it was very hard to get hold of the accent of English and Prince was not that much fluent in the language. Dave was unhappy and told me to think whatever I wanted. Afterwards he told me that Prince was quite clever than the teenagers in England. I kept mum. We started looking for a school for him. At last we were able to find a good one, but we did not have enough money to pay the fees and the price for uniform and books. So, we waited for a fortnight.

My sister died in the middle of December so I had to go for her funeral at Mauritius. I had to spend all my money there. When

I came back, I could see that they had used my laptop in my absence. When I checked the websites, I was shocked to see that someone had watched porn in that. I asked who was with Dave watching them. Dave told me that it was he who watched that and he did that by mistake. I was fed up and told them that none of them was going to touch it without my permission.

Since Prince came to live with us, he went on according to his own wish. He did not know how to behave and I tried to teach him. Sometimes I could see him with valuable furniture of the house. One day I opened the television and saw that he had changed the box settings. I kept my patience with him. But one day, I found him with my new T.V. set and I could not control my anger. I told him that there was a rule in the house. He was free to do anything but he must take permission before doing so. He said it was fine with him. Gradually he learnt to make coffee, say "Good Morning" and sleep with his pyjamas on. But that was only for a few days. After that he started opposing me by giving the excuse that his dad had told him this or that. One day, I summoned both of them and asked them the truth. Dave said that he didn't tell anything to him and he was sticking to the point that his dad had told him. I knew that one of them was surely lying and I wanted to know who it could be.

Dave and Prince looked at each other and then Dave told me that there was a misunderstanding and it would not happen any further. I did not say anything to them as I had faith on myself. I was sure that I would change Prince one day as I had changed his dad. By the end of December, Prince was totally out of control and he was not co-operating with me. He started destroying my decorations. He broke a lot of things as he was very careless. When I was not able to bear any further I called up his dad and coaxed him to ask Prince if anything was wrong with him or if I had committed some mistake. He could not behave with me in the way he wanted. I said that I loved Dave a lot and so I thought that his son would be like my own son but he just poured cold water over my expectations. He had to behave himself properly if he wanted to live with us, otherwise Dave would send him back to Mauritius. I was not ready to keep an ill-mannered boy with me, and said that if he acted right and good, he would be happy, else we would be forced to send him back, and we would look after his maintenance and studies from here. As Dave was having his own house in Mauritius, it would not be difficult for Prince to stay there. I wanted to know if I had done anything wrong or he was taking the revenge of his mom. Since November, he had given his number to everybody but not me. It was unbearable.

I was irritated so I summoned Dave and told him that Prince's air ticket was going to expire on 6th of January and he would send him back. He said that he had to call his parents and ask them if they were ready to allow Prince to live with him. I said that if they didn't agree, there was only one solution to it. He had to go back to Mauritius and live there with his son in order to look after him. I had already done enough for him and his entire family and was not in a position either mentally or financially to do anything more. He was not happy to hear that and we had a heated argument.

Dave assured me that he would change in future and be happy with me. But I knew very well that he was leading a double life. He behaved differently with me when his dad was present, and it changed when he was alone. We used to watch television together and it was only me who used to initiate the conversations. I used to feel so stressed out when he didn't respond to me. One day I heard his father telling him that he had just two weeks in hands. If he didn't change himself by that time, he would be sent back to Mauritius. He must give his phone number to me as if anything happened to him, I would be the first who would be contacted as I always used to stay at home. He did not pay any heed to his dad also.

Every afternoon, Prince would wake up when I had completed doing all the household chores. He didn't help me even a bit and had no sympathy for me. Prince continued to make my life hell. There was tension in our lives. One day Dave called his ex-wife and told her that Prince was behaving badly with me and he did not give his number. She wanted to talk to him and said that she would have a word with her. She asked him why he was behaving badly and told him that he should give positively give me his phone number. He agreed to do so over the phone, but he did not oblige after he ended the call. I had no clue why he didn't want to give his phone number to me.

I went to my room and did not come downstairs for dinner. They didn't even bother to call me. They had their own dinner by themselves. He came to the bedroom late and did not say a single word to me. Next day too, I didn't have my breakfast or lunch. At about 5p.m he came to the bedroom to look for his passport. He was quiet and I told him that I needed an explanation. He said that his parents were convinced and they didn't want Prince to travel alone. So, his dad was going to pay for his ticket and he was going back along with Prince to Mauritius. Next day, he was not at home at 11a.m. When I called him, he left a message on his son's mobile informing that he was in the city arranging for his ticket and he would be back by 12 noon.

When he came back he told me that he was going back to Mauritius the next day. I asked him for the last time if he had decided everything. I told him to give a second thought as he was having problem with his passport and visa. I kept on grudging that after I did so much for him and made so many sacrifices he was going to leave me all alone just because of his son, and that too without any fault of mine. He left the bedroom quietly and went to the lounge and asked his son to pack up his suitcase. Next day, when my niece came to visit me, I told her that as Dave was sleeping and I was upset, I wanted to go for an outing to freshen up. We started getting ready but didn't go for shopping, as I saw him crying in the lounge. I went to him and asked him the reason. He sobbed and said that he was being compelled to leave me for his son. He loved me so much but he was helpless.

I asked him not to cry as I was going to be the person who would shed tears after losing everything in life. He had his son as a support to him. If Prince didn't like me he would have told and I would not have spent so much. The amount was about 4000 pounds which was not a small sum. I told him frankly that I could not bear someone in my life who had no respect for me. If Dave loved me he would stay back and sent his son alone. I promised to look after him as long as he was not able to look after himself.

I told Dave that I was not that bad and I could try to talk to Prince about his problem. My niece also supported my idea. She said that we should have a mutual discussion and settle everything and the lives of three persons were involved within the matter. Later on my brother-in-law came and he was quite surprised to hear everything. My sister also arrived and all of us settled down to have a talk. We all came to know that Prince had no feelings for any of us at all. He was feeling bad for his behaviour. So we all came to the decision that Prince would be given some time to change his behaviour. He would realise that his future would be shaped well if he stayed in England, and he must understand my position in his life and the sacrifices I had done for him.

But I was given the final authority to decide whether they both would stay with me or not. I had a soft corner for both of them. I wanted a child all throughout my life desperately. So I forgot everything and gave thought of giving Prince another chance. Dave told Prince that if he wanted to stay with me he had to stick to the values and rules of the house strictly and be obedient to me and the most important of all, he must apologise before me for his behaviour. He agreed to all the conditions and promised to be a good boy.

Prince had started going to school after that, and our lives became much easier. I was less stressed and happiness returned to our lives. On the first weekend I taught him how to clean his uniform and shoes and do the ironing. At first, he used to grudge that he was not used to do all those at home. I told him that there was no one to teach him so long, but I was there for him at England as his mother, and I should teach him everything, as everyone in England was supposed to learn everything. It would for his benefit only in future. By that time I had saved 600 pounds and with that, we were able to buy an old car. It then became easy for Dave to go to his work and we could go shopping any time.

In late 2009, Dave's sister and her family came to spend a few days with us. One day when we were having dinner, his brother-in-law asked Prince if he was coping up well in England. He wanted to know if he had learnt to speak English fluently. Prince answered back in affirmative. His brother-in-law was quite surprised on hearing that and revealed that he had been living in Ireland for the past three years and was still having difficulty with the accent, whereas the first few weeks were really tough for him. Then how could Prince learn everything so fast?

Prince fired back by saying that he was able to speak English so well that he sometimes forgot few words in his mother tongue. He exaggerated that he even mixed English words when he was talking at home. I wondered how he could tell such rubbish after spending just two months in U.K. I thought he was out of his mind. Next day, all of them went to Central London, and Dave's brother-in-law called me up at home to enquire about the way. When they came back, he told me that they were charging roaming rates on his number as he was having his Ireland SIM. So, I asked him to take Prince's mobile when he would go out next day.

Next day, his brother-in-law again called me up from his own number and I asked what happened to Prince's number. He told me that his 5 pounds voucher had expired. When he came back, I asked Prince to bring the mobile as I wanted to check the balance. He didn't want to show me, and after much coaxing he brought his cell. And to my surprise, when I called the customer care for enquiring about the matter, they told me that the voucher was never activated. I asked Prince where he got that idea of lying that he had himself called the customer care and activated the voucher. I told him that nobody in this world was too clever, and he was too young to hide anything from me. We had to learn things from our elders only. I asked him to change his attitude, be well mannered and one day, his dad would feel proud of him.

On the other hand, Dave's attitude towards me also changed. He was always busy with his work, or he was always feeling sleepy if he had to do night shifts. He had no other work to do. He just went to work, ate and lazed around in front of T.V. He had no time for me. Rather than feeling happy, I started feeling depressed, neglected and traumatised. I did not know why I was living like a servant in their life. I had no entertainment, no support and no one to talk or share my feelings. I used to do the household work, prepare food for them, and think about struggle and money all the time. I passed many sleepless nights often.

One day I was going through the local newspaper and my eyes fell on an advertisement which was for promoting places where one could spend nice time, make friends and enjoy. I thought of going to such places for freshening myself, but my sister was in England for her treatment, and she often used to come to my place. I thought that after she would leave, I would go out. I was unhappy with both Dave and Prince. Whenever I asked Prince to do something or help me a bit with my work, he would refuse over my face as he knew that his father was soundly sleeping.

I tried my level best but could change him. If I complained to his dad about his behaviour all he would do was just to shout at him. Dave was no more being patient. Prince was unhappy with his dad too. So I talked to Dave and told him that slapping or beating a child was not a remedy. He would be patient with Prince and make him understand lovingly. Dave said that he was not a sort of person who understood loving words so it was better if he shouted at him.

One day when Dave was at work, I summoned Prince and told him that I wanted to talk with him regarding our lives. I wanted to let him know everything; about how I met his dad, what sacrifices I had done and what hardships I had been throughout my life. I told him how Dave and I met for the first time and in which situation. I said that he had no food and no shelter, and he was always worried about his son and his future. So I helped him, and we got married.

I went on telling how we had fought together so long. I also told him how his father was accused in rape case and his days in prison, loss of tenants as well as customers for him. Even at that age, I had been working so hard just to help his dad in bringing him over our place so that we could be a complete and happy family. We had all our hopes laid on him, and it was only Prince who could help us to rebuild our lives by changing himself. I had great expectations that he would change some day and accept me as his mother as I too longed for a child and I loved him dearly. If he did that, we could be happiest family in the entire planet and everybody would envy us.

I narrated the entire story to him with tears in my eyes. I could not hold back my emotions as I was loitering down the memory lane. But to the greatest surprise of my life, I found that Prince was not emotional at all. He had no expression on his face. He neither expressed his sadness nor happiness on hearing everything. He didn't tell a single word. That day, I realised that Prince was not a normal teenager. He was either traumatised or he must have any problem in his life.

So I asked Dave to bring him to the GP where I had already taken an appointment. I wanted to do the counselling of Prince as I was desperate to know what his problem was. He took him there and they advised Dave to make enquiry at the school if his teachers had noticed something unusual so that they would send him to a philologist. So Dave went to enquire at the school, and his teachers gave the report that there was nothing wrong about Prince. But I was sure that something was seriously wrong and I told Dave about that.

He told me that it was normal with modern day teenagers and I should not worry much. I tried to convince Dave by asking him whether it was normal not to have any sort of expressions on the face. I told him that as long as he had been here, I had not seen even a drop of tear in his eyes. Even if he was not happy with me or had some problem, he would express that in works or by crying, which children of Prince's age normally do. But Dave was not ready to pay any heed to my words and he fired back that I was always thinking myself to be right. There was nothing wrong with Prince and he would behave normally in due course of time.

CHAPTER-16:
Troubles Continued With Prince

One day I asked Prince to clean the mirror. After he was done, I went to check it and saw there were stains on the glass even after he cleaned that as he had said. I asked quite displeasingly whether he was not able to see the marks on the glass. He resumed his rude behaviour and fired back by saying that most probably; it was me who was blind. I didn't know what he felt, but after sometime, he told me that he could not see properly. He also informed that he had requested his teacher at school to shift him to the front row so that he did not face any difficulty in following the blackboard. I asked him if he had told his dad about his eye sight problem, to which he said yes. According to him, he has told his dad about that last week, but no steps were taken by him.

I took an appointment for eye test after two days. I told him that instead of telling his father he could have come and told me, as his dad used to be ignorant of anything in the family. He had no time to care for us. I wanted to make Prince realise that even though he did not like me, I was the only person in England who cared for him. His dad had a mentality which said that your duty is over after you had brought you son to your place. Unlike other fathers, Dave was never curious to know how his son fared in the class; if he was he was enjoying his stay at England, if he was having his lunch or dinner in time or if he was good at health.

But I tried to be a dutiful mother and cared for him in every possible way. I had taken an appointment with the Specsavers.

So, Prince went there and underwent his eye test, and within five days, he received his spectacles. He didn't even feel the urge to thank me once. When he came back home, he was coaxed by Dave to thank me which he did reluctantly. I continued to be unhappy with his behaviour. Sometimes I used to get angry with him and shout, but afterwards I regretted. I wanted him to be my own son, so I used to go up to him and apologise so that he came down for dinner and be happy. Dave always used to say that Prince would change some day and become like him, and would start liking and loving me and pay me the same respect as Dave used to give. If he didn't come to our expectations then he was sure to be a monster. Dave assured me that Prince liked me but didn't want to show that off.

One day I planned to go out for shopping, so before going out, I opened my purse to check the money and was surprised to see that 20 pounds were missing. So I went to the bank and withdrew 260 pounds for my shopping. After I was done, I replaced the amount with another 200 pounds so that I could have 260 pounds in my hands at the end of the month. When I came back home, I saw that 260 pounds were missing and that had been replaced by 40 pounds. I put that money in my purse, but next day again the same thing happened. 40 pounds vanished from my purse.

Dave was at his work for all day long. I was very angry and upset with the stealing case. I was pretty sure that it was no one else but Prince as he was the one who had the chances of doing so. But I knew if I complained against him before his dad, the only thing he would do was to shout at him or beat him, and even drove him out of the house. So I felt it would not be right to tell his dad, and I did as I thought. I kept the entire matter supressed and thought of fixing a particular amount of pocket money for Prince. I tried to be more careful from then onwards and did not keep lot of money in my purse. Next day, I called Prince and gave him his pocket money. I reminded him that it was the 8th of March, 2010, so he would be receiving his amount on 8th of all the months.

That week, I noticed that Prince was not taking a help with the sandwich, and by the end of that week, I had to put all the filings and toppings of sandwich in the garbage bin. I was not happy at all, and what added to my worry was that Prince started coming late from school for few days. I thought it would be right to inform his das so I did, and told him that Prince was coming home at 6:30 p.m. every day, whereas he was supposed to come at 4p.m. Dave summoned Prince and enquired about the matter. Prince lied flatly that such a thing happened only on Thursdays as he was playing basketball, so he came back at 6p.m. I was dumb founded at the tantrums of a child and told Dave that I did not know what more to say, but he could be sure that I was not lying. I asked him to keep a watch on Prince, or make him understand that he was doing wrong, otherwise he would turn worse. I did not forget to mention that if he did not change, I was going to send him back to Mauritius by the end of that year.

Dave did not say anything that day; neither had he tried to defend himself or his son. I asked to go to sleep and get up by 5p.m so that he could judge the situation himself. He did not pay any heed to my words and went on sleeping. At the end of June, I paid the fare of three tickets to Mauritius. We were scheduled to leave on 14th of December. I still had students at our house and we could save for the holidays. I again warned them that if Prince changed himself, only then I was going to bring him back to England, otherwise not. However, Prince gave a deaf ear to all my warnings, and went on with his tantrums. He used to behave in such a way as if there was no one else and he was the master of the house. He shouted at my little nephew every time he came to play at my place.

One day, Dave, his cousin and Prince were trying to fix a radio cassette in our car. After much difficulty, they gave up. Dave came and told me that they were not able to fix that and he might require changing the cassette. He said that he would do it some other time. After sometime, when I went upstairs, Prince acted rather abnormally by closing his room door over my face. I wanted to check with his actions so I went and opened the door. Suddenly he came running to the entrance and guarded my way and said that he would not let me go inside. I was in a state of anger that I would surely go inside and check as I had all right to go inside. So, I got inside forcibly and to my surprise I saw that he was sitting with some tools and the radio cassette opened.

I could no longer control my anger, and came down hastily. I started showing my wrath to Dave and asked him to go upstairs to witness with his own eyes what his son was up to. I also told him to make Prince realise that I was the owner of the house so I had every right to go anywhere around the house. I could hear Dave shouting at Prince from downstairs, and when he came down he said that Prince was just out of his mind. As Dave's cousin was present at that time, we did not comment any further.

He continued to behave with me in such a manner as if I was just a weed of no use in his life. I could very well understand that he used to do so purposely in order to make me feel at every moment that the house he was living in was owned by his father, and I was no one in their lives, nor I had any right on him. One Saturday, while he was cleaning something, he dropped a prized possession of mine and broke it into pieces. I had treasured it for a long time so naturally, I was quite upset. Seething with rage, I told him that I was not going to give chance any farther, and from that day onwards, neither was I going to grudge at him, nor complain to Dave. He had just a few months more to do all those mischiefs and he can live his life according to his wish.

I felt sorry afterwards but I was helpless. Though Prince was just a child of 15 years, his nature was too bossy. He had the idea that he could rule anybody he liked. I knew he would turn worse at Mauritius as there was no one there to look after his actions, but I had to think of my as well. Earlier, I had led a life of much suffering so I wanted to enjoy my life to the fullest as I had got a chance of doing so.

One day I asked him to go to the shop for buying some milk. When he returned from the shop, I was cooking so I asked him to keep the change on the table. He accomplished that and went away. Later when he was with Dave in the kitchen, he complained to him against me by saying that I did not give him money for buying things for his cooking lessons next day. I was not aware of all those. I just saw Dave a bit upset and unhappy. He did not even bid good bye and left for work early. Perhaps he avoided telling me anything as I was with my sister. So we called in Prince and asked him if he had done something which made his dad upset. He said that everything was fine and nothing happened.

Next morning when Dave returned from and we were having our breakfast, Dave broke in the incident before me. I was taken aback and could not imagine how shrewd Prince could be. I realised that he could go to any extent to harass me. I told Dave that nothing of that sort happened and Prince had lied to him. I asked him to believe me as I was saying the complete truth and even told him to ask Prince in the afternoon when he returned from school. He would come to know then who was wrong and who was right.

When he came back from school, both of us were watching T.V., so we didn't ask him anything. Later when Dave asked him whether he was speaking the truth he replied yes and I had refused to give the money. His dad started shouting at him. He then gave the excuse that may be I didn't hear him asking for money. I was surprised at his ability of lying and changing words in a flash. I asked when he asked me for money. He said when he came to keep the change, he asked for it. As I didn't reply, he told Dave the entire matter.

I was sure that he needed to buy something that was why he was playing that game. I told sarcastically that if he had to buy anything he would have asked for money before going to the market, and not after coming back from there. I added to the point that I was not that sort of a person who would refuse give his son some money. I could not even think of doing so to my enemies. He was entrapped in his own net. Finally he admitted before his dad that he was lying against me all the time, and I was speaking the truth. Dave got so furious that he threw his cup of coffee towards him. I somehow stopped him and asked him to cool down. I told him that we could both get into trouble if he beat Prince as child abuse laws are quite strict in England. Moreover Prince was my step son, so blame would come on us only.

I asked Dave to leave Prince on his own way. He had no need to tell him anything as I was determined in ending him back to Mauritius in December. Dave agreed with me and stopped saying anything to him from that day. I knew that Prince would be a free bird and would do anything he liked to me. But the truth was that he had already been doing so since he came. I felt deep pain inside and cried almost every day. I wanted Prince to be a good person. I loved him like my own son, as I had always craved for a child who would treat me as a mom. But the situation was such that I had to fear of losing both Dave and Prince or only Prince. Whatever it was, it was difficult to digest. I just had the faint hope in my mind that one day,

Prince would understand my value and would love me and come back to me.

Days passed and our lives were not usual as before. It turned bitter with time. Both I and Dave were worried about Prince's future if we got time; our only topic of discussion was how we could change Prince. Dave even told me on day that may be we both were too much imposing up on him. He would be given some space. One must be nice with me. We also could not ignore the fact that as I didn't have a child of my own, maybe I didn't know how to bring up a child properly. But we didn't have the clue how to approach a child who was so introvert by nature and refused to share anything with anybody.

Maybe he was frustrated as well as angry with his parents. Both of them left him at quite an early age. Dave came to England and his ex-wife looked after Prince for 5 years. Then she handed over him to Dave as she was going to marry another person, and that person did not want him in their lives. Prince must have felt very down and nourished the idea that he was unwanted in the lives of everyone who dwell in this planet. So, at the end of the day, we could not reach into any solution and we had to remain helpless.

Dave continued to be busy with his work. He used to do night shifts four days a week, and above all, he used to sleep more than he worked. I wondered how he could be so cool even after knowing about the insecure future of his son. I started feeling that I was the only one who used to worry and be unhappy. I often pondered over the fact what happiness I got actually by marrying Dave. When I recollected the past, I could see that I had gained only pain and nothing else.

To be very honest, I also started feeling that the love which I used to have for Dave in my heart was no more responding to my thoughts. He just said in words that he loved me and only pretended to be a good husband. But when my bad times came and there was no one to support he was just spending his days in peace. I made up my mind that I would not let my mind to be vulnerable anymore and bring back Prince to my life. If I had to leave Dave for that, I was ready for that too. Somehow, I felt that I could be happy and well off if I lived alone.

Summer came and went by. We did not go for any outing. I got bored and depressed by staying at home all day. By mid of October, he came back home from work and told me that he had hurt his shoulder with a patient and he was suffering from pain. So he took an appointment with the GP and went to see him. After returning, he informed that he had been advised to take rest for a few days. So, he took sick leave at his work place. After about 15 days, he started going to work, two or three days per week. I was surprised and asked him that they could make someone work when he is on rest. He told me that I was not aware of the rules of the hospital, and he continued to do so for the entire month of November. At the end of the month, he brought me his roster so I did not ask for an explanation any further.

Whenever we got time to talk, it would be about Prince; whether he would be going back to Mauritius or not. Every time, Dave used to say that he would send back Prince to Mauritius and he himself would stay with me and care for me. Though he said he loved me very much and he needed me so he could not leave me, I no longer felt the same warmth or feelings as I used to feel before. I could feel that he had no time for me. He stopped caring for me. He talked to me only when he needed something or he wanted to. He always locked himself up in the bedroom upstairs, remaining busy all day with his newly bought iPhone. Whenever I went upstairs to talk to him regarding that, he would say that I was putting too much pressure on him. Often he would go to meet his friend two or three times a week. Whenever his friend came over to our place, they would talk among themselves privately, not bothering to make me a part of that conversation even though till then I was legally his married wife and I owned that house.

One day when I went to my laptop, I could see that somebody had used it at 12:53a.m. What on Earth could be their need that they had to use my laptop at such an odd hour of night? So, I called both of them and demanded the truth. Both of them said that they had no clue about it, but I was very sure that it was one of the two who did that. So, I told them that next morning, I was going to check the website last browsed. Hearing that, Prince confessed that it was he who used the laptop. I told Dave that he had seen his son's actions, and I demanded that how I could live with Prince or trust him under the same roof. Dave didn't say anything to him. After that day, Dave didn't feel any need to rebuke Prince.

Finally 3rd of December arrived and I thought of inviting all my sisters and other relatives for dinner over my place on my 57th birthday. I received a card from Dave which had something uncanny about it. He had written that he would like to wish me a happy birthday. I don't know why but I felt something wrong about the words "would like". When I opened Prince's card, I saw a letter was attached to it. I went through that and saw that he had apologised for his wrongdoings. He had written that I was a wonderful woman and he had no intention to hurt me, and if he had done it, I must forgive as I was very special to him.

ON 12th of December, I called in Dave and informed him that I was going to tell Prince to pack all his belongings, as he was not going to come back with us. Dave told me it would be as per my wish. I told him that I had no other alternative. I tried to be friendly with Prince and worked up to my level best to change his manners and habits, but he was not the least co-operative. I said that I loved Dave so much and I did every possible thing in order to bring Prince into our lives, but he had poured water over all my intentions. So, I had no other options left. It would be better for all three of us.

I said that it was Prince who deserved my love more as he was a child and that too, a child without his father or mother with him. But he was too arrogant to understand anything. He never even tried to understand me or be least supportive to my efforts. I have lots of expectations from him as well as Dave but both of them failed to cope up with them. That night I cried but no one tried to hug me. Both Dave and Prince did not bother to speak to me or comfort me. They had their dinner on their own and felt no need to call me. I asked Prince not to go to school next day, as we would be travelling after that day. We had a lot of work pending so I wanted Prince to stay with me and help me.

That night at about 11p.m, Prince came to my room and asked for permission to go to school next day. I asked him the reason behind that. He told me that he was required to return something important to the principal. So, I granted him the permission. But later on it stroked my mind that I could not let him to go to school as he was not a person who could be believed up on unconditionally. He was such a person who was always ready to do anything possible so that I got into trouble. I didn't want the situation to become unfavourable just on the eve of departure. So, on that night I told him that I could not let him go. Still next morning, he woke up early to go to school. But I told him sternly that he would not be allowed to go so he got helpless and went back to bed reluctantly.

Next day, we were scheduled to fly to Mauritius in the afternoon. After we reached there, I saw that all of our relatives, including his parents had arrived to receive us at the airport.

CHAPTER-17:
The Final Blow

At the time we reached Mauritius, my sister was living in England; so her house was empty. So Prince went with his grandparents to stay at their place and I and Dave decided to stay at my sister's house. That night when we were talking about Dave, I said that I was not going to tell his parents about Prince then only, as Prince's birthday was approaching. It was on 23rd of December. Dave supported my idea and appreciated that.

Next day, the two of us went to his parents' house and spent the day there together. Later on that day, they came to stay with us. The next day, we went to the beach for an outing and after the day was over, we dropped them at their place and came back. Prince too accompanied us. He was busy planning for his birthday. We had decided to celebrate the day on 24th of December, along with Christmas Eve. On the scheduled day, Dave's parents called up and asked us to go over to their place as they had decided to celebrate Prince's birthday over there. So, we all went over there for the occasion. It was nothing special; just a family dinner. All the family members on my in-laws side other my father-in-law and mother-in-law; his brother, sisters and their kids were present. We had our dinner together and stayed there for the night. Next morning, we received a bad news that. It was the sad demise of the mother of Dave's one of the friends. From the talks, I came to know that the friend shared quite a close relation with Dave so he had to leave for his place in order to attend the funeral later on that day.

So, he woke early that morning at 5a.m, and asked me to get ready so that he could drop me home early. I came back with Prince and Dave's nieces. When Dave returned from the funeral, he went to his parents' place and brought them to our place. We all had a good time that day and everybody was happy. That night when we went to bed, Dave thanked me for the umpteenth time. He said that he was very grateful to me for celebrating his son's birthday even after I was aware of the fact that Prince did not like me. He also said that his parents were also happy with my actions. I said that I just listened to my heart. It was against my nature to hurt people. I want everyone to be happy so I was happy to organise the event.

The next day we again went to the beach with his parents for an outing and came back home quite late. So we headed to my mom's place for having our dinner. When we came back and were ready for going to bed that night, I told Dave that I was going to tell his parents everything about Prince's actions and the decisions we had taken regarding him. He said that it was okay as we had to say the truth and let his grandparents know everything someday.

When we went over to his parents' place the next day, his mom and grandma were there. Dave requested me not to tell anything in front of his mom as he feared that she might not be able to bear such complaints against Prince, as she was his grandma and had quite a soft corner for her grandson. I understood what Dave meant so we came back without telling anything. After coming back, he informed me that his friend had arranged for a prayer post to his mother's death. Dave wanted to be there and he went. I stayed back as I had planned to spend the day with my mom and sisters. Actually we had the plan to have lunch together on the occasion of my niece's birthday.

Dave came back at about 5p.m in the afternoon. We had invitation to a birthday party that evening. So, we there together and when we came back Dave hailed me as darling and informed me that his parents were coming to meet me next morning. He said that they wanted to talk with me regarding the matter of Prince. I had a plan to visit my aunt's place with my mom next day so I asked him why he had told them to come next day only. I told him that they could talk to him only. Why was I required? He told me that as the decision was mine, they wanted to have a talk with me. I agreed and asked him to tell them to come a bit early so that I was not late for my previous engagement. He told me not to worry as they would be at our place on time.

Next morning at 7:30a.m, his dad called at our place and informed us that they were on their way. We had not left bed till then, so after receiving the call, he shook me and asked to wake up and get ready as his parents would be reaching in few minutes. So I woke up and got ready to face them. We were standing in the balcony when they arrived along with Prince at our place. His mother came and told me that they wanted to know the reason why I had decided to leave Price back at Mauritius. I asked her about the person who gave her the information. She said that it was no one. Rather when she saw all the belongings of Prince inside the suitcase, she herself had guessed that something was wrong. So they had come to talk on that topic.

At that, I turned towards Prince and said that he had three persons by his side, and I was standing alone having no one to support me. I asked him to confess before his grandparents all his mischiefs and wrongdoings. I told him not to be scared and say only the truth. I asked if I had ever behaved badly with him, or if I had made him feel uncomfortable, unwelcome and uneasy at my house to which he said no. I further asked him to say the reason to his grandparents why he was beaten at that tender age. If he had been a good child and acted accordingly, he would have been loved by everyone.

Before he could answer anything, his grandma sprang up on and accused me of not behaving well with Prince. She even said that I was a bad woman and not at all a good mother. I did not know how to treat a child. I was shocked at her words and I just could not make out how she could utter those words even being aware of my sacrifices for his son and grandson. She went on saying that she had come to me to let me know that they were not going to keep Prince with them. As they were already retired, they had to look after each other so it was not possible for them at any cost. She said that it was Dave's duty to think about the well-being and future of his son.

I was so distressed that I failed to say anything more. I just started shedding my tears and I began to ponder when I was bad with Prince. I had always liked and loved him like my own son and what I got in return. No respect, no love; just tears and tears. Moreover, Dave's mother did not even take a second to accuse me with such a grave mistake which I had never even imagined of committing. As our neighbour was loitering in her garden at that time, my mother-in-law became kind enough to stop the family drama then! She said that it was time for them to go back and it was our duty to think over what to do. She came to give me a goodbye kiss even after all those incidents. I repelled from her and went inside. After all I was not good as an actress like hers. She accused me of being a bad person sometime before and then she felt like giving me a goodbye kiss! I was not made of stone that I could bear anything. Even Dave kept mum and gave supported his mom silently.

I went upstairs and locked myself in my room. I shed my tears as much as I could so that my heart became a bit light and I was relieved. I stayed there for one hour. Dave did not come to console me. When I came downstairs, I saw him standing in the balcony. He was crying. Still I did not feel like saying anything to him and went quietly to finish my household chores. He came to help me in cleaning the utensils as if nothing abnormal had happened. After finishing washing and other works, we set ahead for my mom's place. From there we visited my aunty. We stayed there for dinner and came back home late that night. When were ready for bed, he told me that he had received a call from his dad and he had to go his mom's place. His dad wanted to talk with him about finding a suitable school for Prince. The wound that I receive from them was afresh in my heart and mind and I told Dave that it was not possible for me after the morning incident to go there. But he was completely free to go as they were his parents and he also had his responsibilities towards them as well as his son.

So, he went there next day and came back at 5p.m. He said that he was feeling very tired after the hectic day due to journey and scorching heat of the sun. He told me that he was going to take a bath and then take rest. So after he got fresh, he slept for two hours. After he woke up, we watched T.V. for some time and then came for dinner. He broke in the news that his mom had been admitted to the hospital due to stress at that age and he had to go to pay a visit to her.

So he went that day. It was 29th of December, 2010. After he stepped out of the house he did not call me even once which he usually used to do to know how I was doing with everything. Sensing the abnormal situation, I felt something was seriously wrong even with Dave. He came back the next day at the same time he came yesterday. He told me that his mother was released and was at home. He wanted to spend the night at his mom's place with his parents as on Christmas Eve, we had spent the day at my mom's place. So, on the eve of New Year, he wanted to be with his parents. I said that it was fine with me and agreed to stay with my mom for a night.

He said that he would turn up in the evening as we were invited for dinner T my mom's place. On 31st of December, when we were having breakfast at our table, I told him that it was the last day of the year. So, I wanted to get everything settled so that we could wake up next day and start a new life with new pledges in the New Year. He said that he wanted that too. He also said that he wanted to let me know that he was going to his parents to have a final talk with them. He would tell them that if they did not want accommodate Prince with the, they should leave his house and shift downstairs.

I warned him not to do anything of that sort in front of Prince as he was already 15 years old. He had already gone through many downs in his small life which had made him hard hearted already. Then, if he saw his dad behaving unnaturally with his grandparents, it could be a mental blow to him. As I was aware of the actions he could take, I could easily imagine the consequences after that. So I asked Dave to request his parents nicely to let Prince stay with them. It was just providing him a room in their house as we had already decided to carry on his expenses on studies and everything. Dave assured me that he would do that only and he hoped that his parents agreed with him.

I then told Dave that I was going to tell him what plights I had gone through in the past few months and how I had felt. I had been unhappy because he had been ignorant about me lately. But I had my thoughts to myself and did not grudge on anything. I told him truly that I felt he did not love anymore and he had someone else in his life; he had not changed his habits even then. He told me earnestly that he loved me and did not want to lose me. I was the first priority in his life and he did not ever want me to be unhappy. He wanted to spend the rest of his life with me. He assured me that since February 2009, he had never cheated me on my back and pleaded with me to trust him. He promised me to start a new life in the New Year and for that reason only; he was going to have a final word with his parents.

I was relieved and started laughing freely after a long time. I told him that though he had made me unhappy all the year along, he had made me happy with his words on the last day at least. I forgot everything and we completed our breakfast together. He asked me if I had any work to do. I said that at first, I needed to go to the bank, and then drop something at my sister's place. He asked me to get ready as we would be going together. So we went out. He told me that he was not sure if there was enough petrol in the van. So, at first we went to the petrol pump, where we took petrol in the tank, which was almost full. He laughed and said that he could not make out as the indicator was not working properly.

We went to the bank after that and then had a lunch of fried noodles at the market. He then bought a water melon for my mom and then we headed towards my sister's place for dropping the thing. When we came to our house, we both were feeling quite tired as it was a sunny day. He told me that he was going to travel by bus for reaching his parents' house. His neighbour was throwing a party so space would be scanty and he would not be able to park the car. I was bit surprised and asked him to go over to his friend's place and park the van there as his house was not far from his friend's. But he refused to do so and stuck to the point of travelling by bus.

As he was having his shower, he requested me to iron a pair of his trousers and shirt for him. I readily did that. He was wearing a pair of jeans which I gave him and a shirt which my sister gave him as a gift on his birthday. When he got ready, he told me that he was thinking to bring a new set of dress. I supported his idea and asked him to do so as next day was 1st January, and it was a tradition in our country to wear new clothes on the occasion of New Year. He told me remorsefully that he didn't think he had got another new set. I asked him to check his wardrobe. There he would find a new set of black trousers and a white cotton shirt with the tags still intact. I told him that I had bought that for him.

After checking when he came back to the lounge, he was overwhelming with joy. He hugged me and said that he had liked the gift very much. I was like an angel to him and I did care for him just like a baby. I never forgot anything and kept everything ready at hand. He was grateful to God for having me as his wife. Before he went out, he informed me that he had taken Rs.10000. He handed Rs.7000 to me and said that he was going to take Rs.3000 along with him. I refused to take the money as I did not require it next day. So I asked him to take the entire amount with him in case he needed the money that night. I also said that we could go somewhere next day after he returned. But he would not listen to me and hid the money in the kitchen. He took his bag and bade me good bye. He asked me to care of myself and promised me to call once he reached there.

At first he went to my mom's place to give the water melon to her and to inform her that I was going to come to her place for staying that night as he was going to his parents' house to spend the New Year's Eve with them. When I did not receive a call from him even at 5:30p.m in the afternoon, I myself called him up. He received that he had reached there just then and he was facing a problem with his battery. I asked him to put that on charge. He told me that no one had a charger like mine. Whatever it was, he would try to charge that. He asked me not to call him. He would be sending me a message at midnight.

At midnight, I again called him but his mobile was switched off. I thought that he might have problem in charging the battery and therefore, it was flat. So I gave up trying. At 3a.m in the morning, I received a message from Dave which said that he would like to wish me a great New Year. He wanted me to be happy, successful and prosper throughout the year. I was a bit surprised on seeing that 'would like' again. I didn't know why but it gave me the hint that something was wrong. Anyways, I did not let the bad thoughts rule my mind and felt that I was worrying without any reason.

Next morning was the first day in the New Year. I hoped that Dave would call me but they were shattered. I did not hear anything from him. I thought he must be busy with his parents so I did not call as I did not want to disturb him. But when it was afternoon and still silence on his part, I could not hold myself back and called him at 4:30p.m. The phone rang but no one answered. I again tried to call at 5:35p.m, and the same thing happened. I went to take a shower after that, and when I was in the bathroom, the phone rang at 6:30p.m. But I was not able to answer the call.

When I came out, I could see that I had a message from Dave. He had written that he had a heated argument with his parents. They were not at all willing to let Prince stay with them. So he had decided to leave me and stay back at Mauritius to look after and take care of his son. As my passport, tickets and other important documents were still in his bag, he would turn up on Monday or Tuesday to give them back to me. I was speechless and shocked at his move. I felt there was no ground under my feet and I would fall very easily. For a few minutes, I stood absolutely motionless, and after I recovered I tried to call him but his phone was switched off.

I somehow got ready and went over to my mom's place for having dinner. When it was 9p.m and still he had not shown his face, everyone started enquiring about him. I showed his message to my niece to which she told me that she had talk with me about something very important. All my relatives also told me that they wanted to talk to me. They showed me some photos of Dave with another woman on Facebook. Dave's profile did not bear his real name. I was shattered to see four different photos of Dave, and in none of them he had his wedding ring on. I could not even think that to be true. My relatives informed me further that Prince had been chatting with that woman since August, and they came to know about all those since August. They kept mum as they had felt I could be able to bear the hard core fact that Dave had again been cheating on my back. They did not want to break my belief that Dave loved me dearly.

Bur for me, I got the greatest shock of my life when I went through the name of that woman. It was none but Laka, Dave's girlfriend since 2008. So, the case became very clear and transparent like water to me. I then knew that he was playing that game and was having a double life with me. My relatives advised me not to do anything but just wait for him till Monday or Tuesday as he had mentioned. On 2nd of January, his parents came and dropped an envelope for me with my mom. As per my instructions, she told them that I was not with her. She advised them to go my sister's house which was not very far away. They refused to do so as they were in a hurry to leave. She also asked them about Dave and Prince. They said that Dave had an argument with them regarding accommodation of Prince and he had left their house and went to stay at his friend's place.

As soon as they had left, my mother called me and informed me about the entire matter. I tried to call Dave but it went on ringing and I received no answer. I tried his father's number and the same thing happened. I understood that they had started to avoid me completely. So, I tried from niece's mobile number which was unknown to them, and that time his dad received the call. When he heard my voice, he said that they nothing else to tell me and they did not want to talk to me. I fired back that I had every right to bring police to their place but I would not do that and ended the call. When I opened the envelope, I found there were three tickets, my passport, visa and all the bank cards Dave had taken with them when he went to their house.

I made up mind not to bother about him any further in my life. He had given me only pain and nothing else. At the crucial stage he had decided to leave me then why I was going to worry about him. I tried to call his friend's number too but that call went unanswered as the rest. On 4th of January, I received a call from him. I answered the call but on the other side, he kept silent. I controlled my temper and told him nicely to tell me anything he wanted to. Still he kept mum. I told him that I didn't have time to wait until he spoke all day along as I was busy with other works. He texted me a while later and started to pretend that he loved me. He framed his lies and started vomiting them! He said that he was not well and was having some problem with his network. He was still busy in looking for school and work. He would call me later.

I could no longer control my temper hearing his lies. I got upset and texted him back saying angrily that I had found out his photo with his girlfriend Laka on Facebook. I knew that he cheated me again and he was having a double life with me. Both he and his son were of the same category. I asked him not to worry about me any further as I was happy to get rid of a person like him. I wished him luck with his girlfriend and said that I hoped Prince would be also happy with Laka as I had seen he had been chatting with her since a long time. I did not have any clue why they did that to me. And from that day onwards, I heard no more from him.

On 6th of January, I sent two letters with his aunty, one for him and the other one for his dad. I sent the photos obtained from Facebook to his dad and that was the real face and character of his son that is, to stab someone on the back. I told him sarcastically that as I had been very bad to Prince and treated him badly, I was sure that he would be happy with Laka. She would obviously look after him and take care of him well. I asked his dad one last question that had I been his own daughter, what he would have done. For Dave, I wrote a few words along with the Facebook photos. The letter went on like that I was sure that he did not want to give an explanation any more. If he felt that it was the husband's duty to advise me what to do with the house, he was free to do that. If he wanted to give any advice, I would decide on what can be done. I wished him good luck for his future with Laka and Prince.

No one would be as ungrateful as him even after knowing what I had done for him. Had it been me, I would have committed suicide thinking how bad I had been. But he was a monster and that was why he was not able to understand the human values. I waited till 12th of January but nothing eventful happened. I went back to England on that day as per my return ticket was booked. I went to our house and started crying like anything. For the first time in my life, I felt like killing myself. People might think that I was crying because I lost him. But the fact was that I was crying on my own folly. I made another wrong choice for which I was repenting then.

I came to know that he had been in England since 2nd of January. He had been in the house just for his work pass, other documents etc. He had taken a few letters which my sister collected from him and handed over those to me. She told me that she had seen one envelope from DVLA and she was sure that it was his driving license. I said that it was not possible for him to obtain license as he had not yet then passed the driving test. My sister told me that I was too straight to understand anything. I would know later. The car was parked in front of our house.

CHAPTER-18: *The Way I Feel*

He was a cheater, thief, liar, abuser of trust and I do not know what more adjectives I shall use to describe his nature. He was something more than what I have said just now. But if ever, he gets the chance to go through this book of mine, he will know what I mean to say. Even if you feed a dog even it is not yours, it will wag its tail whenever it will see you. But Dave's mentality was even lower than that of a dog. He spat on the same plate on which he used to have his meals. I lost 2000 pounds on the house I had rented but I had no other option other than that. Now I am residing in a small one bedroom flat, but my life is now more peaceful than ever had been. I don't know how long he will continue to run away from hiding his face from me. But honestly speaking, he has granted me a favour by doing that. I don't want to see his face ever.

I hate him now. Deliberately I hate him. I used to love him dearly and he was my life once up on a time, but he is just an evil shadow in my life. I used to be his shadow according his words only, but now I don't want to have his shadow and even its effect on my life. If you give a rotten bone to a dog, I am sure that it will not taste that, but Dave will still rub his nose and mouth against it. He will surely taste that as he perhaps believes in the idea that a born cheater will continue to be cheater only. I may sound very funny but he is like that only. He is the king of lies and abuse, and I want to let him know that his entire family, his parents, siblings and his son all are like him. They are of same nature and follow the same principle of abusing anyone's trust. They might dwell in this mortal world but they behaved like aliens. People might think that I am saying these low words against him and his family because I got betrayed by him, but this is not true. I know him very well, how mean he is and that is why I am expressing these after a long period of suffering.

The first thing I had to do was to look for a small one bedroom flat as the rent of the house I was living in was too high. I shifted to my new house and gave the landlord my address. I was worried about how to shift all the things including his belongings to the new house. I should not have spent so much on his clothes, tickets and everything. I did not even imagine that my life would be turned into this after I came back from my holidays. I had a lot of things to do. But whatever I did, I knew that I would be happy without him. I used to keep myself very busy all day long in order to make my heart forget him. I started giving everything on charity as no one lived for no one. But in the bed, I could not hold back my tears and often wet my pillows. I prayed to God to help me out and make me forget everything.

Gradually I learnt that Dave lost his job in the hospital much before. Of course, he deserved that. He did such mean things there that I am sure they must not have any other alternative other than dismissing him. I came to know that one day, he went to his manageress and told her his brother had met with an accident in Mauritius and he was hospitalised in a very critical condition. So he wanted 15 days leave as he had to go there. He was granted that leave and I am the eye witness, so can swear by the name of God that he had not gone out of the house in that period. In 2008, he again applied for leave. That time the excuse was the imaginary death of his uncle who lived in France! He was required to go for his funeral.

Again in 2009, he went to demand leave for 15 days as according to him, his mom was admitted in the ICU with a severe stroke on account of loss of his brother. So they granted him leave and when he came back he told them that he had to perform his mother's funeral as she passed away. I had booked for our holiday from March, 2010. One day he came and told me to change the journey date from 10th of December to 14th of December as he was granted leave at that time only. So, I did not mind changing the date. But from the middle of October, he was on sick leave and just one week before travelling, he came and told me that he was not sure if he could go.

He did not mention in front of me that he was on sick leave, but just said that they may not permit him to go as he was not fully cured of his back pain. So he had to go to the PR office on Monday to confirm if he could go or not. On Monday afternoon he came and told me that he allowed him to travel. But I now can hear a complete different story regarding that. He had told the hospital that he needed leave for attending the prayer in Mauritius on his mom's death anniversary, whom he claimed to be dead in November, 2009. So they granted him leave even he was on sick leave.

I can't even imagine how one can say such types of things about one's relatives who are still alive. I have never seen someone so much narrow minded. One day in March 2011, he met a friend of mine, and he told her that he was in Mauritius. He had come here just a few days back as his brother-in-law died and for that reason he had to stay here for long. He even told her that his son was still at Mauritius. After a few days, that woman again saw him at the bus stop and was surprised. So she told the entire matter to me.

I realised that he will never give up his habit of lying exclusively. I am now happy and proud to be the person I am now. In spite of the fact that I had spent eight and half years with that man, I had not let myself to become like him. I am proud that I am still following my own principles, the teachings which my parents imparted up on me, and moreover I am thankful to God that he had helped me in recognising the evil in Dave, though late. He often used to tell me that I am very stupid and immature. Everyone takes advantage of me due to that reason. But now I can scream and say that no one else, but he is the only person who did that to me. He abused my trust brutally. My other two husbands did not play with my emotions like this. Dave had appeared to be sweet and stabbed me on my back. It hurts more if you are given a blow by your loved one. Dave did that and I hate him for that.

No one is like him. He is a burden in people's lives and on this planet. I should have left him dying in 2002, and let him die in the jail. I took pity on him but I regret that now. He is destined to go to jail for being a fraud and he must die there only. He does not even deserve a glass of water before his death. One day he will surely plunged into such an end; I know that God will listen to prayer and on that day, great sinner will be deceased from the Earth and people will be saved from him. I am eagerly waiting for that day. I know I have to be patient and have faith on God.

I know I cannot be happy totally with him but I don't want him either in my life. I shall never be able to forget my past. It will continue to me, and even after almost three months have passed since he left me, I still cannot believe that he never loved me. But it is true that he married e and used my money just to get settled in England and to look after his son. Otherwise how can one kick out someone from his life on the very first day of the year who had done so many sacrifices for him. He wiped off everything in just a second.

He was having one foot on the grave when I met him, and now he had completely forgotten me and chose his son. It was the same son whom he had left at the age of five years without any maintenance. It was me who had taken all pains and troubles and fought for bringing his son. I was the one who looked after him and cared for him. And now when his son is fifteen years old, he is saying he will look after him. I just wonder how long his son is going to be with him and what he thinks of his dad. How can a son respect his dad who has no respect with him?

The case is like something that Dave had even let his son know about the presence of a mistress in his life, otherwise how could Prince chat with her? I am just pondering over the fact that he had a wife at home and a mistress outside. When he used to say that he was going to his workplace, his son was aware of the fact that he was lying and was going to sleep with another woman outside. In the next moment, he used to see his dad with his wife on the bed. What can be the impact of all those on a child of fifteen years. Into what kind of person he will grow up? As he is now staying with his dad, it is very probable that he depicts the character of his dad only.

Anyways, I do not have any interest in their lives now. It is their life and they only know how to carry on with it. There are various sorts of fathers in the world who keep different traces of their fatherhood in this mortal world. I just hope that this special dad and son relationship between Dave and his son remains the same for the eternity! My aim behind writing this book is not to tell readers that no men can be trusted or they possess love only in bed. But I want to let my readers know that I had been a special and dutiful wife all throughout my life to all the three of my spouses.

EPILOGUE

My first husband, Goldie was obsessed with kids, and he chose to be with another woman just for kids. He said he loved me, but I don't know whether he was true as when I asked him to hire a surrogate mother; he turned me down saying he wanted a child with love. Does love mean to have physical relation only and produce children? It might be so. I am still searching an answer to this. He asked me to stay in his life just as a mere doll, and I could not accomplish that.

My second husband, Brainie was simply obsessed with money. For him, money was everything and other things served no importance in his life. He wanted me to be his money machine and after spending seven years with him, Dave came in my life.

Dave, my third husband was obsessed with sex. For him marriage was just the license to physical relation freely. Whereas for me, marriage is a very sacred relation; a relation which I believe can be nurtured only with love, faith and happiness. Again love is not a simple as it sounds to be. It is the mental and emotional attachment between two persons. You cannot go before two or three persons at a time, and tell them that you love them.

Before you tell a person that you love him or her, at first give a thought whether you have any respect for that person and if you can keep him or her happy. Have some love in your heart for the person with whom you are sharing a physical relation. I am so confused after so many incidents in my life that I still do not have answers to many questions. I am writing this book and I hope earnestly that the readers will help me in finding answers to these questions:

I don't know if I had been married too many times.

I don't know even if any one of my husbands loved me.

I don't know if they had just abused my life and my trust and kicked me out of their lives.

I don't know if I had sacrificed too for their well-being and future.

I don't know if anyone can put any limit on love.

I don't know if it was my fault to believe on them unconditionally.

I don't know if I had been foolish all throughout my life.

I don't know if this is the consequence of my life which I deserved from them.

I don't know if I had been a bad wife and not able to come up to the expectations of my husbands.

I don't know if as a person I am good or bad, or I am still childish.

After passing through all these incidents and too many experiences in my life, I have realised one truth in my life that it is not right to love someone else more than you and amongst all the husbands; the best was the second one. Even though he was obsessed with money, he left with a lot of things for thriving in my life. He also imparted up on me a good knowledge of savings and expenditure, and the ways of the world. He helped me to become a British citizen without hesitation, and he used to say that I had been very good to him.

The third one gave me a lot of hope and promised me with happiness but ultimately just abused my trust. After his aim of bringing is son to England was fulfilled, he kicked me out of his life. He thinks that no one will ever come to know about his past, but I know that there is no rubber existing in this mortal world which will help him in wiping his past. I don't mind about what he did to me, because he will surely realise his mistake and Mr Dave, let me tell you very clearly that I will be strong that day and will not forgive you at any cost. I will just see to it that how you can thrive without money, support and friends. I want to see who gives you sex and fun when your wallet becomes empty.

I am remembering now his fake words. He told me that he loved me and as I did not have a child of my own, I would love his son dearly. His son would too like me as I was a wonderful woman in his life. Surely, his son would too find me wonderful. And now, it is coming to my ears through other people that he had told them I did not look after his son well. I beat him and I was a bad mother! What a fate! I have one request to the world, if ever you are in pain, and you are thinking of taking painkillers, please think of my life once and you will not need any extra painkiller.

I consider myself to be a painkiller in his life as I was the one who absorbed al his pain and troubles and gave him just happiness. No one is immortal in this mortal world and I will not be living in this world forever, but I want the story of my life to a practical example to many for decades. Maybe it was not possible for him to accept me in his life. He led a double life with me for eight and half years, and after that when he was not able to continue any further, he chose one and threw me out of his life. He would not have been able to do that without hurting me. I am thankful to God that he made a choice.

God is great. Maybe I was not aware before that I did something wrong. The thing which I had, I have and I will continue to have forever is my faith on God. I know he will help me choose the right over the wrong; he will look after me and will help me to forget my past and continue with my life. I know he will not turn down his true devotees and will return everything to me that I lost; my happiness and taste of life. Maybe it was my fault that I had been overconfident regarding the relation between me and Dave, that we will walk through all the up sand downs of our life together. Was I too possessive about him?

Whatever the situation was, I am happy that it is no longer like that now. Whether it rains or snows now, I know that I am all alone in my life and will continue to be so.